PRAISE

"Sixty minutes before she steps in front of a speeding van..." Thus begins Claire Polders' smart, sophisticated, unrelentingly candid examination of female adolescence and womanhood. This collection makes its mark, intellectually and emotionally, with prose that's alive and electric and exquisitely distilled. Polders uses time—wields it actually—as a narrative drumbeat, marching her characters over the jagged terrain and uncertain landscapes of sex and seduction and coming of age. Told from individual and collective points of view, the stories portray not just the pain and rage and sorrows of living as a woman in a patriarchal society, but also those moments of transcendence, transformation, and self-becoming. *Woman of the Hour: Fifty Tales of Longing and Rebellion* is a brilliant and necessary collection for our times."
KATHY FISH, AUTHOR OF *WILD LIFE: COLLECTED WORKS*

"The riveting characters in *Woman of the Hour* are full of desire, anger, regret, and darkness. Their fragmented lives are tough, but their grit inspires. This brilliant collection makes you love people again."
GRANT FAULKNER, AUTHOR OF
THE ART OF BREVITY: CRAFTING THE VERY SHORT STORY

"I simply devoured each stunning piece. Part travelogue—journeying through history, place, and the complexities of the female experience, revealing sensual exploration, seduction, exploitation. Part poetry—blending food, nature, and metamorphoses both animal and human. Claire Polders' flash collection is an exquisite celebration of the whole, the real self, and a call to action for the girl, the woman, and the crone. With quiet intensity and intellectual depth, each flash unveils vivid portraiture of what it means to be a fully alive, thinking, and yearning being."

Jolene McIlwain, author of NPR-Book-of-the-Year *Sidle Creek*

"In *Woman of the Hour: Fifty Stories of Longing and Rebellion*, Claire Polders illuminates the universal in the particular, capturing the essence of how it is to be female in prose that is exquisite in its precision, at once tough and lyric. Her protagonists walk the tightrope of life, navigating the delicate balance between tensions—independence and connection, societal expectations and a sense of self, responsibility and desire—in an ongoing and eternal search for meaning versus mere existence. Ultimately, there are questions, but no definitive answers: 'To live, she has learned, is to wonder,' says the Woman of the Year. Each story in this collection is like a Godiva chocolate, dense and delicious: Dig in."

Sarah Freligh, author of *Other Emergencies*

"In this brilliant, lyrical collection of flash, Claire Polders shines a kaleidoscopic light on the mystery of being human in a female body. Like figures in a stained-glass window, the many selves she explores assemble into a whole self—contradictory, passionate, and so protean they find it 'a delight to live in a world where you can witness the dawn multiple times.' Polders' vision, universal and probing, invites the reader to ask the eternal question 'Who Am I?' and guarantees you will not be disappointed."

Thaisa Frank, author of *Heidegger's Glasses*

About the Author

Claire Polders grew up in the Netherlands, studied philosophy, lived in Paris, married an American in Italy, and now slow-travels the world as a nomad. She's the author of four novels in Dutch and co-author of one novel for younger readers in English (*A Whale in Paris*, Simon & Schuster). *Woman of the Hour: Fifty Tales of Longing and Rebellion* is her debut story collection.

clairepolders.com

Claire Polders

Woman of the Hour

Fifty Tales of Longing and Rebellion

www.vineleavespress.com

Woman of the Hour: Fifty Tales of Longing and Rebellion

Print Edition
ISBN: 978-3-98832-163-3
Published by Vine Leaves Press 2025

Cover design by Jessica Bell
Interior design by Amie McCracken

We cannot read the darkness. We cannot read it. It is a form of madness, albeit a common one, that we try.

—from *Bluets* by Maggie Nelson

Contents

Woman of the Hour
Woman of the Hour - 15
Dawn - 19
Lost Animal Identities - 21
Playground - 25
Bleeding Girls Initiation Ritual - 27
Speaking of Ovid - 31
Her Face in the Glass - 35
A Tasting of European Chefs - 37
Because I Cannot Travel in Time - 39
The Spider and I - 41

Woman of the Day
Woman of the Day - 45
New Leader - 49
Copycat - 51
The Path to the Future - 55
Dance Partners - 57
The Next - 59
Swan Lake - 61
Classic - 63
Liabilities - 65
If You Think Stars Can't Clap, You're Not Listening - 67

Woman of the Week
Woman of the Week - 71
Snails and Oysters - 73
Double Life - 75
Repairs - 79
Battle of Brushes - 81

Floris, Fate, and the Friendly Stranger - 83
Lost and Found - 85
Saving Lives Left and Right - 87
Ugly Thing - 91
The Hardest Thing - 93

Woman of the Year

Woman of the Year - 97
Five Forbidden Friends - 101
An Interesting Case - 105
Undeserved Gift - 107
The Mind Reader - 109
Guillotine - 111
Closed Circle - 117
Attic - 121
Inner Thief - 123
What I Pack for a Sleepover at My Sister's House - 125

Woman of the Century

Woman of the Century - 129
Mirror - 133
Rivals - 135
Retracing - 137
Stella Is - 139
Absent Reflections - 141
Office Women - 143
Omission - 147
The Cost of Living - 149
Looking for a Place to Die - 153

Acknowledgements - 155

WOMAN OF THE HOUR

WOMAN OF THE HOUR

Sixty minutes before she steps in front of a speeding van, she blenders bird seeds with berries for her vegan twelve-year-old, who dirties their kitchen each Saturday for some type of raw bake-off but cannot get up early enough on school days to mix her own shake. As a mother, she practices patience. Her smile tempers yet never quite masks her discontent. She looks haunted by a tampon jingle, smelling her own rancid blood.

Fifty minutes before she loses her breath in a death-threat flash, she secretly dictates a dentist appointment into her husband's calendar and sets up a reminder for seven days ahead. She should neither startle him with a sudden visit nor let him know about it for too long in advance. As a wife, she protects. If she lets his anxieties spin out of control, the whole household will suffer. There are limits to what their healthy diet can cure.

Forty minutes before the driver hits his brakes with the power of blind rage, she verifies whether her mother's scheduled caregiver has checked in on time to drive her mother to the oncologist. As a daughter, she's at a distance. In her early forties, when she herself experienced a cancer scare and filled bowls with vomit, she stopped trying to gain the love she had missed as a child. She's a confident woman. If only because she refuses to be in a story in which readers see her flattened under a misery the weight of a truck.

Thirty minutes before small-town bystanders look up from their phones and applaud her, she sends an emoji-rich message to her bestie, who suffers from envy as though it were a chronic back pain. As a friend, she condones. Each time she meets with such a special person in her life, she feels as though she's spreading a picnic blanket under a blossoming jasmine tree and is handed a life-prolonging elixir. The pleasure she derives from holding hands can be greater than from sex.

Twenty minutes before she spots the family of ducks crossing the street in a line, she calls her new team member with detailed instructions on how to prepare the brand-identity presentation later that day. *Last but not least: The smell of fresh coffee is key.* As an employee, she goes beyond the call of duty. Not in the hopes of advancing her career, but because she cannot bear to witness catastrophes.

Ten minutes before she bursts out laughing at the thought of being a brave woman for the sake of seven ducks, she unintentionally catches a vagrant's eye and drops her loose change in a held-out hand. As a heroine, she is pathetic. Who has time for saving the world? Her father, apparently, who moved to Oaxaca at the age of seventy-three and became an activist for the Mixtecs. She turned the news of his departure over in her hands, like a sharp thing picked up from the grass. Is it true that she has his jaw?

At the time of her near death, she steps off the sidewalk into traffic, not seeking to shatter her bones, yet distracted by the unexpected image of herself as a broken vase, a woman in jagged pieces. The van screeches to a halt in a cliché she fails to notice. There's the stink of burnt rubber, and a memory flickers, ghostlike. As a child, she was a theater talent and still whole. She would stand on the makeshift stage of their shoddy living room rug, performing a self-written play in a self-made costume, hair in a ponytail hidden beneath a wig, acting out all the parts and getting applauded by the merry adults, including her mother, for so convincingly being anyone but herself.

DAWN

She wears the desolation of what we know to be death like a robe, the light in her body extinguished. She's the first to return, and we receive her in style, holding her armlessly with our eyes. We wash her feet, whisper fruit into her hands. Her bed is made with the smoothest leaves, pillows of solace and air. We would keep her aloft on our breath if we could. Would suck out the harm and lift her mind, replace the memory of rods with resilient snapdragons.

She masks herself in silence at first, in open ears and closed lips. What she does with her mouth is like a seal, so the cold of her world won't infect us. We swallow our dread and mirror her, pressing our words flat against the sides of our throats. There's a ravine at the end of her tale better left unprobed. Days later, when the speaking begins, her voice will be as thin as the rest of her, too transparent to reveal who she has become. Her words will at most hint at the woman she once was, someone who needed no silence, had nothing to hide.

When shadows lengthen, we grow alert, watch the sun descend into darkness. We huddle around the fire, hunting and judging, never closing all our eyes all at once. The ambiance calls for howling dogs and stifled cries, yet what we hear are the crickets ringing false. However nameless, we know it's out there on the edge. Our fears become legible; our solitude, intimate. Backs turned to the phantom parade, we tell each other stories of dreams realized, believing in our innocence as in a magic spell. In our curved lives, we force things to point forward. This is how we win.

In the dark, she leans into us. We lend her the moon above the lake and let her look through our imagination. Solidarity is resistance. There, we say, our eye in the sky, its craters waiting to absorb your tears. But what restores her to life even more than our intentions is the half-light of dawn, floating down on us like a caress, painting her face with violet and cobalt. Our vigilance wanes. The death from which she returned always comes for us at night.

LOST ANIMAL IDENTITIES

The first time I turned, I was seven years old. I sat on a hard mattress in my grandmother's guest bedroom on the second floor with a man I truly liked, the clean-faced husband of my grandmother's sister. The man and I were in the habit of making excursions together on his bicycle. Together, we dove into the village swimming pool or watched swans flap their threatening wings when we came too close. That afternoon, however, while my grandmother and his wife were downstairs, chatting in the quarreling manner that was their style, the man and I were alone in the bedroom for a reason I cannot recall. He touched me or held me or handled me for another reason I cannot recall, but what I do remember is that I turned, from an obedient child into a sly fox. My fur was a gorgeous bristly red and made him gasp. In his confusion, I squirmed from his hands with one smooth lie—*I'm hungry*—and fled the room. The metamorphosis didn't last long, my fur gone before I reached my grandmother, but the fox's trace in me forbade me forevermore to sit on the rear end of the man's bicycle.

I played on a sunny field of grass when I turned a second time. I loved wrestling with my older brother, my youngish step-mother, with anyone who tossed me around without hurting me on purpose. Wrestling was a way for me to connect and simultaneously release anger. That day, I was wrestling with my scout leader while a semicircle of eager girls surrounded us: They waited to take my place. He was an unattractive guy, we all agreed, and I doubt any of us were sweet on him, and his age, twice our own, put him off-limits even for our fantasies, but male attention is male attention. I wrestled with him until one of my emerging breasts got in the way. Instantly, I turned into a snake who showed her fangs. He released me just as quickly and backed away, lest I bite. I hissed so loudly that other scout leaders rushed toward us and put a stop to the weekly wrestling for good.

I turned many times in the years to come. The neighbor who peeked at my naked mother suntanning in our fenced garden made me grow a turtle shell. The boyfriend pushing my boundaries freed the buzzing bee in me. The cook at the retirement home where I delivered meals birthed my inner porcupine when his hands bumped into my butt cheeks more than accidentally possible. The flasher on the Paris metro met my toxic frog and flirtatious professors of all stripes gave me wings. Whenever men were heading to places where I didn't want to go, I turned.

At twenty-one, I turned for the last time. Men didn't stop bothering me, but ... you'll see. I lived with a guy who wanted me to have his babies, and because he called me selfish for my wanting to have my university degrees first, we fought a lot. One day in the kitchen, he tried to shove me out the back door onto the closed-in patio, where it was snowing. I had been there before, cooped up without a coat, and wasn't looking forward to waiting for his mercy again in the winter cold. So the bear in me broke out. My partner was a big guy, yet surprise won me the advantage. He stumbled backward against the cupboard. The sound of clattering things. I raised my paw to slash him open, but just before I struck, I caught my reflection in the oven glass. A woman was standing there with her thin arm raised. No bear in sight. I roared.

PLAYGROUND

They come for coffee when it rains and overstay their welcome. They come alone or in pairs, leaving mud trails on the floor. They come with earbuds, attitudes, and hard mouths. She knows by now: Rudeness travels with power.

Today, one officer sits across from her at the kitchen table, his hands more nicked than the wood. He eyes the cans on her counter. “That’s a lot of beans.”

She nods. “For the food bank. The church put out a call.”

Although she knew him when he still wetted his bed—he and her son painted dragons together—she does not know him now.

He rubs his sweaty neck. “Hope they’re not doling that stuff out to the wrong people.”

She shrugs, denying responsibility. Most officers consider her a Friend of the State, because of her war-hero son, her voting record, but suspicions can turn into facts overnight. One accusation will put her under surveillance.

“More?” She lifts the carafe. Kindness, true or fake, is never wasted.

He holds out his cup as though their meeting is normal. Ever since the regime issued the 11th Order, and citizens threatened with arrest went missing overnight, officers have been patrolling the neighborhood. Rumors circulate that even conservatives have opened their doors and turned homes into shelters.

She pours coffee and testifies: no suspicious behavior, no confidences overheard, nothing to report. His microphone buzzes like a dying fly. At times, she confesses things that are vague yet of interest, just to prove she's playing ball. Privacy is a peacetime luxury.

After the officer leaves, she locks the door, draws the curtains, warms up the soup, and prepares the tray. She hums a made-up tune. Headaches belong to the past now. She can write to her co-conspirators all night and still be up at six to bake bread.

"You've buried your grief," old friends say.

The family of refugees awaits her in the basement. A woman and her two girls. A brother-in-law. The basement is gloomy and damp, but not unfriendly. In a better world, it would have been her grandchildren's playground.

Once a week, on Sunday morning, she takes the family out into the yard, where they sit with their faces like sunflowers turned to the light. In a defiant stroke of foresight, weeks before he was killed, her son built the shed that protects them all from view.

Bleeding Girls Initiation Ritual

We arrive in the dark on the shortest night and cluster away from the pyre. We are nameless and unsure, bleeding without a wound. We count: forty of us against three of them. Still, we feel outnumbered. We rub our cramping bellies. Woodsmoke makes us cry.

The Leader yells from his soapbox, demanding law and order. His voice pierces our bodies like needles. We stop shuffling and straighten our spines, our muscles tight with tension. All around us, nocturnal insects hum, drawn to our youth, our flowing blood.

Form a circle, the Leader shouts. We squeeze ourselves around the fire as the Bully squeezes us, our butt cheeks and tender breasts. Silently observing is the Boy: Everything that happens here tonight will go into the Book of Men.

The Leader tells us to step forward, one by one, and relinquish our dreams to the flames.

We don't move. We barely breathe. We turn our heads only to look at one another and at the sky. The full moon glows ghostly white, like a broken promise. We are dolls of straw and cloth. We don't know how to become real.

The Bully shoves one of us in the back, separating her from us, the circle. She stumbles forward, looking blurry. The swirling smoke steals her shape, her boundaries.

Relinquish your dream, the Leader shouts.

She digs into her skirt pocket, removes a finger puppet, and observes it like a jeweler would examine a precious stone. She glances over her shoulder, back at us. We smile to help, but our smiles are fake and therefore useless.

She faces the pyre and throws her dream into the flames.

Ashes whirl up. The blaze whips our skins dry as bone.

The Bully spits in her face, pushes her away, jerks another one of us toward the heat. As she flinches, so do we.

Bigger! The Leader shouts.

She feeds the fire with a paper plane.

Orange flames shoot out toward us. We withdraw, yet the Bully forces us back. He speaks with kicks and punches. Violence appears to give him pleasure, as though it's chocolate melting on his tongue.

Bigger! The Leader shouts again. You must sacrifice your *biggest* dream!

When the third of us steps forward, the Boy faces her and says, Please do as they say. It will be better for all of us.

We don't understand his pronouns "they" and "us," but we understand his warning. He seems to sway between two worlds, eyes brimming with pity. Still, he returns to the sideline, his silent position, safe.

One of us removes her shoes and surrenders them to the fire. We watch the rubber curl, then melt, inhaling the fumes. We feel like animals with a paw caught in a trap. Sparks of desperation singe our throats.

We act more quickly now, poked by the Bully or braving the flames on our own. Dreams fly like birds from our hands. We give up a ring, a sharp pencil, locks of hair, a pair of transparent gloves. We throw in an egg fertilized by the wind. Set alight a future child. We bite off a fingertip, surrender an intuition, fold our wings and let them ignite.

The flames keep being hungry: The Leader wants more. We watch our treasures burn, heat charring our faces, until one of us is about to gouge out her eyes.

No, we sigh.

And she stops.

We feel it happening. A pause, a freeze, a doubt. A refusal of pain. It rises as a song in our bodies, starting low, then surging out of one mouth. It's a call to arms. Our arms.

No, one of us screams.

Her voice, our voice, is a storm that changes everything. It fills, then clears the night. The moon, at last, delivers its power into our minds.

The Leader yells, the Bully beats, and the Boy blinks, looking from the men toward us and back. He could be our brother, our future son. But he could also become the bully or the next man claiming to be in charge.

The bravery of one of us spreads like a virus and infiltrates our veins. Now there are two of us screaming, four of us, fifteen, twenty-one, thirty-six, forty. Finally, we understand: Our initiation is a revolution.

We reach into the fire and retrieve our dreams, slap them around to extinguish the flames. We blow life back into the cinders.

The Leader is still yelling when we drag him off the soapbox, stuff his mouth with moss, tie him up with spider silk, and drop him into the woods where the animals will piss on him to lessen his stink.

Our last fears fall away from us like stars.

We tackle the Bully and sing to ourselves—a chorus of encouragement. The Bully thrashes and flails on the ground. His back carves out a pit that fits his body like a grave. We refuse to grant him a last wish. We close the grave.

When we come for the Boy, he's nowhere to be found. We go after him, high on revenge, but once we spot him in the bushes, begging for mercy, we make him our witness: Our victory deserves to be seen.

We dance around the fire, ashen hands in the air, ready to accept the power that is naturally ours. We throw one another names to try them out. We are Saraswati and Antigone and Scheherazade and Joan and Cleopatra and Eve. And we are Fatima and Jing and Camille and Alysha and Maryam and Tamar and Lex. The starry sky seems too small for our elation.

At dawn, we turn our backs to the pyre and triumphantly march home as a pack, carrying our dreams like banners. We are women now, each unique and all together. The earth along the way resembles a freshly born planet, with the sun on top of everything, as rich as gold.

SPEAKING OF OVID

The first time I became myself, I sat talking to a man I barely knew. We were side by side on a too low sofa, sinking into one another, falling out of time. There was a party happening somewhere in another world.

Once the metamorphosis was complete, I recognized myself with pride: There I am, I thought, this is me. The incarnation lasted only a short while, no more than ten minutes I would say, but the experience was so empowering that I knew I could no longer live without being myself on a regular basis. I leapt to conclusions immediately. This man was special. Perhaps, if I spent more time with him, he could turn me into myself for good.

Don't think I was elated. I was annoyed. Why this man, this pseudo stranger? He wasn't smart or funny or sensitive or exciting or anything like that. I had no business getting hooked to a person like him and much preferred to have found myself on my own, which shouldn't have been so hard to do anyway. I don't wear wigs or false eyelashes. I don't even own a push-up bra. I'm fully human, with a human face, and am generally considered to be an adult, so go figure.

Still, the first person who forced me to inhabit myself appeared to be this pudgy man with washed-out eyes. I sat talking to him at the far end of a dinner party, halfway drunk and lost between boredom and indifference. Or perhaps listening is the proper verb; I remember clenching my jaws and staying pleasant. Then a chill announced a change and my senses sharpened. Something was brewing. I could feel it happening. My true self was taking shape. It was like in a dream when you're first and third person at the same time, observing yourself. This may sound contradictory, being yourself outside yourself, but I tell you it's possible: I watched how I became the woman I was meant to be.

And who was that? A willful woman, apparently, the opposite of the people-pleasing girl this man took me to be. The hands on my lap were capable and reliable and totally my own. They flexed and tightened into fists at will. Did the man notice my transformation? Should I call him a prick? Perhaps he noticed how my comportment during dinner was different from how I later behaved, closed and defiant, although I must say that most men aren't that observant. He also never mentioned it. He kept talking about Narcissus and Echo while invading my personal space. Was this why I had transformed? By being myself, complete and whole, there was no room for him inside.

It's a valid theory, because this man I barely knew was the same man who had expressed his hunger to sleep with me. He had not even made the effort to fool me into thinking he cared about my life. No questions about my career or my mother's health or my opinion on climate change. He boldly stated, while we were being introduced during the aperitif, that I was sexually potent—was that the word?—no, compelling, yes, sexually compelling, and that if I ever felt the slightest desire for him, I shouldn't hesitate to make it known so he could act. But, he added, if I didn't feel that desire, it was fine, too, because most women simply didn't see him in the role of Adonis and he was used to that. Why burden a woman with guilt when all she had done was awaken his lust?

Not that I was entirely innocent, of course, judging from the flattering cut of my dress, but still, innocent enough for him to be an adult about it. There was no reason in other words, according to him, that the two of us couldn't have a pleasant conversation about the latest translation of Ovid. I admit, his soliloquy over bloody steak and broiled potatoes had been tolerable. He spoke not only about Orpheus and the Muses, but also about the rape of Proserpina, especially after the strawberry ice cream. We were on the too low sofa by then. Passion is impatient, he said and smiled. He could easily imagine abducting me. Wink. Wink.

Was that a whiff of sulfur? Or the sour tang of fermented grapes coming from the man whose mouth was full of Bacchus? He was expectant, this man, wanting me to render myself impersonally receptive.

By the time the sinking and falling began, with half his weight on top of me, his physical presence demanded my response. What should I do? Because I didn't feel like transforming myself into a tree or a taurus or a wave of chilly liquid, losing all means of expression to accommodate a lover-god, I simply became myself. I said no. NO. Not going to happen. I denied him the act of sex, now and in the future, an act that I was sure would not be pleasurable for me. The thought of sex had crossed my mind, however, the possibility that I would give in to him out of pity, fall victim to that guilt he had mentioned based on the flattering cut of my dress. I had briefly considered taking on the mistaken responsibility of satisfying the lust my body had roused in his. Much to my regret, I had done such things in the past, as recently as several months ago, in fact, when giving in to a roommate I didn't want to lose as a friend had seemed less consequential than thwarting his misdirected, broken-hearted affection.

But that night, on that too low sofa with his weight on me and poor Proserpina on my mind, I decided that this man would not be having his way with me. It wasn't possible to open up to someone who made me so defensively myself.

Her Face in the Glass

Each time she looks in the mirror, she sees her eternal guilt written on her face, a net of thin lines drawing the picture of another woman, a bad woman who has abandoned her husband and child to seek professional fulfillment. Still, she never avoids her reflection, not consciously at least. As unbecoming as this guilt is, written on her face like that, in wrinkles and grooves, it motivates her to continually improve upon herself. The choices she made should be justified. All she gave up should be compensated by the greatness of her work, so that regret—ubiquitous and unending—will never gain a foothold in her life. Others may turn around halfway and go back, but for her a change of heart remains forbidden.

She is a good surgeon, no doubt about it, one of the best in her field, her colleagues assure her. But as she stands there in front of the hospital room window, looking at the young man who is her son, unconscious in bed, hooked up to machines, she sees her own reflection and thinks of his naked navel, the perfect small hole at the center of his body. How he was once separated from her by strange hands, the umbilical cord cut. How her own hands mere hours ago held the scalpel, sliced through his skin, opened him up, removed the bullets, and stitched up the once perfect hole. And her face in the glass wants to know: Is she good enough?

A Tasting of European Chefs

South

Hours slip past in moonlight and summer dresses, sandy and rustling. She watches from the terrace by the shore as he scrubs his outdoor grill yet does not scrub himself. His first note is green with olives and bold with desire, perfectly salted. When she opens her mouth, a blend of flavors pours in, peppery and wet. Tension drains from her body until she's light in the head. He can lift her now and hold her weight, pushing into her with an appetite she finds delicious. *Did you see the stars?* he asks once her feet are back on solid ground. She leans into his neck for one last bite.

East

On a business trip in Prague, months after the Berlin wall came down, she gulps vodka straight from the bottle, hoping to kill the germs that must have colonized her throat from all the French kissing she's been doing in the horrible corridors of the Soviet building where she found a dirt-cheap room. The kitchen where he fixes the same Special of the Day, every day of the week, is right below her. The Czechs are eager kissers, deep kissers, jealous kissers. After he has licked his peach parfait off her lips, he forbids her to sexually socialize with others. His skin smells pungent like his food, an odor of potatoes, bitter herbs, and laundered socks. *Don't you think it's boring, the same special every day?* she asks. Offended, he lights a smoke. *You're here to tell us that we want the stuff we don't need,* he says. She dresses quickly to remind him that she's not a keeper.

North

They feast on smoked lamb and fried bread, let the excess fat moisten their lips and fingers. He's full-bodied with a protruding stomach and nothing tentative about him. With the snow piling up outside like white down, there is every reason to stay in bed, especially when that bed is lined with sheepskins. His hungry mouth glistens, saying that the trick to keeping warm in the dark is to be a gourmand. He goes down on her. She straddles him. He bleats and pushes her into the wool. For a long while, they cook together and caramelize, and when she finally falls asleep on his plated chest, she sweet-dreams about love.

West

He shines with innovation, flambéing, sous-viding, foaming, his kitchen a wink of hot promise. But his style of mating does not deserve a star. On the crumb-free sheets in the impersonal room behind his restaurant, she escapes her boredom with eyes closed and her mind traveling, opening her palate to dishes previously enjoyed. He cannot imagine what tickles her taste buds while he stirs her broth. With her culinary memories alive in her body, she is always and never alone.

Because I Cannot Travel in Time

It would take an odyssey to reunite with our mother, a journey on a ramshackle bus, three planes, a slow-speed train, and a final tram to bridge the twelve thousand kilometers separating me from the place where we grew up.

It would take all my luck and/or all my savings to exit the warm country where I've been hiding and enter the cold nation where we were born. As you might remember, I tend to overstay my welcome, and my identity has expired.

It would take my deconstruction. To leave, I would have to relinquish the pain that kept me captive all these years, and without this pain, I would fall apart. A stranger would need to pick up my pieces, put them in my smelly green suitcase, and send me on my way.

Alternatively, I could swallow enough pills to numb myself, forgetting how you swallowed whatever I gave you, be it milk or lies or fentanyl. But I fear I would join you prematurely.

It would take stealing a shovel at night, digging into the earth, and wrenching open your grave.

It would take all your magic and/or all my tears to transform you into the beautiful breathing sister you always were.

Alternatively, you could wait for me on your tombstone, smiling or snarling, resurrected by the familiar mothball smell of my green suitcase traveling your way.

It would take me carrying bony you on my shoulders like I did in the dunes when we were young, or it would take you carrying pieces of me in your arms from the cemetery to our home.

What image would soften our mother into forgiveness? Perhaps you better go ahead alone and leave me waiting in your now-open grave. Would she … would you come and find me?

THE SPIDER AND I

When in the early morning I see a spider in the house, I don't squash it like the woman I used to be. Instead, I stagger backward on instinct, then lean forward with intent. I greet the alien creature as though it's a prince in disguise honoring me with his presence. The spider has something to say to me, which shouldn't be surprising. We've met before, you know, the spider and I, in different incarnations. We've met in cold kitchens and hallways, above beds and dusty bicycles, even on my skin at times, still damp from recent sleep. Most meetings began in horror and ended badly. Let's not sugarcoat my murders: The woman I used to be has blood on her hands from the life that scared her to death. Now, I listen to the spider and its webbed words, weaving my shroud or wedding dress from its silky strong threads. I have trained myself to be patient—who knows a spider's true intentions? The creature may wear glasses like me or rub two of its forelegs together as though washing the next bite like a raccoon. Such a clean creature, the spider, black with innocence. The woman I used to be closes her eyes as I stick out my tongue and wait for the prince to climb into my mouth. Why live in denial? When I see a spider in the house, I know the future is near. No matter how many doors I slam or double lock at night, the future will arrive the next day in the early morning like a spider you can either squash or swallow whole.

WOMAN OF THE DAY

WOMAN OF THE DAY

At 6 a.m., she opens her eyes, serenely sated with the essential things she has learned in her sleep. The shower, however, no matter how eco-consciously short, washes most of her wisdom away.

At 7 a.m., her porous mind absorbs the news from around the world. War there, demonstrations here, reports on the declining quality of elder care, burning forests, floods, a minister's lies. She takes bites from her locally grown organic apple while dreaming of (and simultaneously regretting) the days when she was still ignorant enough to enjoy corn flakes and bacon.

At 8 a.m., her bicycle is like a silver horse between her thighs. The air is invigorating, uplifting even, until she joins the city's main artery, clogged by fossil fuel fumes. Each breath steals from her what she gains by using her legs.

At 9 a.m., she delivers a package to a man who regularly receives registered mail and always greets her warmly. A woman who listens is loved. Convinced of the innate interest he must hold for her, he tells her about his favorite pair of scissors. The seasonal flowerpots on the neighbor's windowsill keep her smiling.

At 10 a.m., she accepts a pamphlet from a girl dressed in a pink minidress and over-the-knee pink socks, thinking it's from the breast cancer foundation. When it proves to be a flyer for a budget sushi joint, she briefly feels guilty for having played monopoly as a kid when she was old enough to know better.

At 11 a.m., she pedals fast, fast, fast, silently cursing the people on terraces who laugh as though misery does not exist. She hands over the mail with eyes downcast, no longer able to look into the faces of customers who still believe they're innocent.

At noon, she finds a quiet alley with a blind wall to stand on her hands and turn the world upside down. This is her superpower. Anxieties drain from her like dirty water from a sink. She forgets about the profit impact of terrorist threats and the risks of living in a post-truth world. Back on her feet, she eats her favorite supermarket bean salad on a sunny stoop.

At 1 p.m., legs pumping, saddle pressed against her crotch, she broods over acts of resistance. When will she rise? What should she do besides cutting back? How can she contribute to the greater cause? How is she to make a difference?

At 2 p.m., a car turning right cuts her off. She squeezes the brakes on her bicycle, loses balance, skids to a halt. The car passes criminally close to her front wheel. Her heart clambers high in her chest, as though it's trying to escape through her throat to find safety elsewhere.

At 3 p.m., her brush with death still hums in her body. Like a siren, a melody, an ambivalent wink. In the city's unimaginative suburbs, the wind blows through her hair and the trees … the trees bend and sing with unexpected grace.

At 4 p.m., one shift ends and another begins. She follows her friend's instructions and buys the hamburgers she ethically condemns. Considering the exceptional circumstances, she ignores her itching conscience. Scratching will only make it worse.

At 5 p.m., she parks her bicycle in front of a nondescript house that reveals nothing about what's happening inside, even though it contains three sad little lives hanging on to the one bigger life that is dangling.

At 6 p.m., a recurrent thought pops into her head. Had she made different choices in life, her children would have been about the age of these three little kids she feeds four times a week. Their eyes are like beautiful rebellious lakes in which no one can drown. And yet, what kind of world do they inherit?

At 7 p.m., with the composure of a wartime nurse, she helps her friend take an army of over-the-counter supplements. They both want to believe that nature can cure what medics deem to be beyond hope. But she suspects her friend, too, is playacting.

Home alone at 8 p.m., she cries.

At 9 p.m., she breaks all her rules, betraying who she decided to be. She watches a male-gaze movie, orders child-labor sneakers online, and indiscriminately likes posts. She forgives herself for her weakness. We cannot all be heroes, like we cannot all be prima ballerinas.

At 10 p.m., the beige carpet soaks up her red wine. She picks up the glass and watches the stain as though it were an art piece, a shadow cast by a mysterious object out of sight.

At 11 p.m., she counts her breaths—one, two, sixty-three …

At midnight, she parts the dream clouds with her hands and flies.

New Leader

After Bernhard Christiansen's "Nieuwe Paus" ("New Pope")

This morning, I invented a new leader. I was tired of the old one and thought: I want a leader who is as loyal as my watchdog, Jodie, and as fierce as my cat, Joelle, and who possesses some type of superpower, such as breathing underwater like my goldfish, Jojo. The new leader would be a woman, of course, either resembling my favorite aunt, or that clever lady I often see on TV and whose eyes keep me standing each time I feel tempted to fall into despair. She would have a lovely smile, my leader, a smile that she would never show, unless she meant to give it to you as a present. All men would fear her fingernails. Not because they were painted or as sharp as weapons, but because they made her fingers longer, and therefore her accusations more acute. My new leader would have wild hair, as in *untamed*, as in *free*. She would love to dance and shake her body in a triumph of force. Her voice, too, would be uncaged, allowing her to shout and whisper and sing whenever she felt like making a point, and even when she felt like making nothing. Traveling, for my new leader, would be as easy as spreading her wings like my parrot, Jorinde. And she would never sleep; sleep would be unnecessary. My new leader would absorb what she needed from the opposition, sucking their vapid energy into her own pure wakefulness. Would she have hardened teeth? Nuanced arms? I tried to imagine what dog-eared books she would read in secret, and drew a blank, perhaps because she would carry all the books inside her head, even the ones that had yet to be written. The only complaint you could make about my new leader was that she would be difficult to approach. But that's forgivable, at least in my house. Jodie, Joelle, Jojo, and Jorinde never let me pet them either. Even so, my respect for them is boundless.

COPYCAT

That summer after Jan-Willem left me, I was after Jasper, a twenty-one-year-old surf instructor in Scheveningen who was always in the company of a tittering girl who claimed to be his girlfriend but wasn't. Not spiritually at least, or so I told myself. She was just somebody with tight skin who happened to be dulling his solitude until a yet unnamed future would claim him.

After days of watching his Herculean body ride the North Sea waves, I decided Jasper was my boy. I hired him as my private teacher and humiliated myself into a tight rubber suit. The feel of the cold, wet material against my skin was disgusting. But if Jan-Willem could do it, so could I.

He would have died laughing if he'd seen me, climbing on that waxed board, again and again, my throat raw from salt, my breasts flat as pancakes. How fantastic I was at falling.

"Make gravity work for you," Jasper said. "Gravity is what keeps us balanced."

On shore, his hangout was the surf enclave where SAVE WATER, SHOWER WITH A FRIEND was stenciled on the communal bathroom door. I dreaded the enclave. Tanned, athletic bodies everywhere, a cornucopia of youth. And Jasper's fake girlfriend, of course, watching him as though he were a diamond ring.

The sea bit me. The waves beat me up. But I was determined to make my lessons erotically satisfying, because if Jan-Willem could do it, so could I.

After a week, I saw progress. A hand left longer than usual on my back, a remark about me being fit for my age, et cetera. Not that Jasper was coming on to me, his arrogance wouldn't allow it, but his rapport suggested bigger rewards awaited me if I kept money flowing his way.

One evening, I followed him into the enclave's bar and ordered martinis. His fake girlfriend said he didn't like cocktails and only drank beer. She was wrong. When I massaged his shoulders, she didn't say anything.

I made another move the next day near the showers. "Come over and I'll cook up some mussels," I told my Herculean boy. I gave him directions to my villa, leaving out that it technically belonged to Jan-Willem.

Jasper zipped open his wetsuit and rolled it down to his hips, exposing his six-pack bounty. "Sorry, got plans."

"We don't have to eat mussels," I said.

It was obvious what I was implying—I'd never felt so free, so light—yet he looked at me suspiciously, seeking confirmation. So I gave it to him, surprising us both: I reached forward and cupped his balls inside the wet rubber. Jasper would have pulled back if he hadn't been leaning against the wall. The confusion on his face was priceless. Anxiety, pride, and embarrassment, but above all, excitement: He got hard. Was it really that easy?

I drove us up to my realm in Wassenaar, where the large house waited as quiet as a mountain cave. As soon as we closed the door to the world, we had sex, wild and unformed like fire. If Jan-Willem could do it, so could I.

After that night, the surf lessons stopped. Instead, Jasper came up to the villa whenever he felt like it, which was almost every day at first, then less and less, until I barely saw him more than once a week. It was September and he'd gone back to college. I was fucking a boy with homework.

I didn't complain about the frequency of his visits. Complaining would only put a stop to our modus vivendi immediately, and truth was, I couldn't bear that. I'd taken a liking to the boy who made my orgasms his business as though they made him profit. So I bought him a new surfboard, new flippers, and this did the trick for a while until he coughed up the real problem: His fake girlfriend had moved in with him and his coming here weighed on his conscience. He wanted it to stop.

But you don't care about her, I wanted to say. You never have.

Negotiating, I asked him for one last fuck, for summer's sake, and he generously agreed. That night, I was careful to leave the curtains open, and the moment I had him butt naked in my living room, on my nubuck leather couch, his fake girlfriend showed up just on time and spied us through the bay window. I nudged Jasper, and when he looked up, she ran off.

Believe me, I knew how she felt. But this time, I was the victor. With Jasper still on top of me, I was prepared to feel triumphant. So why this wrenching in my gut? I felt miserable and mortified, like the biggest bitch in the universe. Jasper must have sensed it, too, because he pulled out of me as though I suddenly repulsed him. He rushed to the door and yelled after her, saying who knows what. Well, I know, but I don't want to tell you because he had nothing good to say about me.

What followed was also unscripted. Jasper and I were supposed to collectively laugh at the fake girlfriend and start loving each other for real. He was supposed to invite me to his estate in Sicily to escape the emotional mess. The fake girlfriend, on her cold side of the world, was supposed to reclaim herself in the meantime and become truculent. She was supposed to fight her ex's lawyer, stay in her ex's villa, and seduce some other woman's man, preferably younger. To staunch her bleeding heart. Prove her sexual power. Feel what it was like to be on the other side. If I could do it, so could she.

How was I supposed to know she would drown herself instead?

Gravity isn't what keeps us balanced, Jasper, it's what keeps us from flying off the earth.

THE PATH TO THE FUTURE

Olivia is not an ostrich. She's ready to deal with obstacles that block her path. Few situations faze her.

Ideally, she removes the obstacle from her path completely, using various tactics that include (but are not limited to) charm, clear communication, patience, logical thinking, intimidation, and, when necessary, force.

If the obstacle is of the stubborn kind and will not yield, she reverts to other, less favorable alternatives, such as climbing over the obstacle as if it were a barrier. There's some victory in this, she feels, like climbing Mount Everest.

Another possibility is to go around the obstacle, but Olivia typically doesn't like doing that. Detours make her feel uncourageous.

Still, detours are preferable to the last resort, which is to turn back. Turning back is letting the obstacle dictate where you go and that, obviously, is a dead end. Unless, unless (jumping from one foot to the other) you can convince yourself that the obstacle on your path is all yours. Meaning: It's there just for you, it has been put there, if you will, with the sole purpose of making you change your ways.

But who believes that? Not Olivia. She's not an ostrich. Obstacles have as little to do with predestination as rain with free will.

So that is why, on this Saturday morning in the fall, Olivia does what she does. She studies the snoring obstacle blocking her path, gets down on her knees, and kisses the man's unshaven cheek. Wake up, Daddy, she says, I have an important audition to go to. When the snoring doesn't subside, she showers, gets dressed, and tries it again. Please, Daddy. She gently rocks the man's body and squeezes his nose. Nothing. She imagines how she will get to the Hogendijk Ballet & Dance Studio on the other side of town if her father won't drive her. Ask the neighbor? Call a friend's mother? Take a taxi?

Olivia raises her voice and warns her father that if he doesn't get up RIGHT NOW she may leave him, for good, may move in with her mother. My entire life is at stake, she says. She pokes the non-responsive man on the floor in the ribs and quickly jumps back to avoid being hit by the hairy arms that lash out at her in a half-dormant, half-aggressive state.

Seeing no other options, Olivia climbs over her soon-again soundly sleeping father. In his bedroom, she steals money from his pants. She climbs back over the obstacle on her way out. She slings tutu, leotard, and pointe shoes in a beach bag over her shoulder, adds an apple to the bunch, and leaves the house.

There are no obstacles on the street. Just taxis. The path to the future lies wide open.

Dance Partners

My small-town modern ballet class competed and won the honor of dancing for the elevation of mankind in an empty field surrounded by live animals. All expenses paid for and eternal fame and so forth. Plus a token of gratitude for each.

We showed up in the middle of nowhere, got undressed and dressed behind the van, giggling and cursing the winter cold. Our costumes were blood-red catsuits, which flattened our underdeveloped breasts and cut into our balls. We were eleven or twelve, tall or plump, of various genders and talents. Pancake is what the lady called the stuff she smeared on our faces—to make some of us look less ghostly, we thought.

The cattle truck arrived and with it came the people in blue overalls. They staked the grounds and fenced our stage. Together with the film crew, they were our audience. We appreciated the shamelessness of their stares despite the discomfort they caused us.

Loudspeakers were installed. Our nerves grew. Then they opened the truck and let the animals out.

Had we expected horses? We'd expected horses. Cats, dogs, rabbits. Deer perhaps.

Out came the pigs. Not cute pink piglets you may want to cuddle, but full-grown hairy hogs.

Zero objections came from our teacher so zero complaints from us. Did I mention we were good kids? With our swift ballet feet, we sidestepped our fears and our disgust.

When the music began and the cameras rolled, we danced our butts off in the grassy field, performing the piece we had practiced for weeks. The grace with which we lifted our legs! The power we packed into our air-pounding punches!

We played with the cameras, smiling and batting our lashes, imagining our faces on TV. We even engaged the pigs, not only dancing around them, but including them in our rhythmic euphoria, never losing the beat. We were animated. We were sharp. For the first time in my life I twirled a triple pirouette, spinning and keeping balance in a triumph of body and mind.

When the music stopped, applause flowed our way. We believed we stood on Broadway. Until we noticed the pig shit caked to our bare feet.

The Animal Protection Agency commercial was broadcasted on a rainy day in late spring. All of us dancers from modern ballet class got together at our teacher's house to watch the commercial air. The living room was party central with a revengeful wink: sausages, bacon wraps, ham sandwiches. For added fun, we even wore our tokens of gratitude around our necks: shiny cowbells suspended from ribbons.

We looked, eyes wide, hoping to recognize ourselves on the screen. Only that didn't happen. We were dancing just fine, gloriously at times, our blood-red bodies bouncy among the dull pigs, but in post-production our faces had been replaced by white skulls.

The Next

The sea is still and yet the tarpaulin above the fishing boat moves as though touched by wind. Nova stops scanning the cove for scraps, victim to curiosity. Could be a stray cat enjoying a secret stash. Could be a man. The smell of brine makes her stomach growl. She checks for witnesses in the dusk and seeing none, rushes down the jetty. Survival means taking risks.

The canvas is blue, her hand stained, and the eyes that take her in when she lifts the tarpaulin are scared and bloodshot. Hiding in the boat is a girl her own age, eighteen at most, but already looking like death. Her smile, for all its good intentions, is chilling.

Nova has never shared her food before, not since she's on her own, and she's unconvinced she should be Miss Generosity now—but look, her hand opens her pouch and offers the girl a fist of bread. While the stowaway eats, Nova examines the boat. There's a mattress of fishing nets, a contraption collecting rainwater in a jar. Survival means being creative.

"I have a shack," Nova says. "And you're welcome to stay there. But don't steal. I'll kick your ass if you do."

"No," the stowaway says. "Too risky. I'd get you in trouble."

So the girl was hunted. What had she done? Did it matter?

They whisper in the dark, getting closer to each other, testing trust.

"What are you gonna do?" Nova asks.

A shrug. A flash of hopelessness across the face. She can count on nothing because she doesn't count. Is not even a person under the new law.

Nova leaves and returns, always in the dark, bringing fruit and kindness. But the days go by uneventfully until she realizes that it's up to her, that she must be the hope.

They make a plan. They plan a route. They pulse with power.

On the night the girl will cross the border on a spot where vigilance is low, Nova brings enough provisions to survive a three-day journey. She even donates her parents' pouch.

They set off under cover of darkness, thick clouds obscuring a sliver moon. They advance side by side toward the gate, alert and confident. But near the exit, soldiers materialize and take aim. No warning, nothing. The girls run, zigzag, and duck, bullets flying past.

When the stowaway is hit in the back and falls, Nova drops to her knees beside her. She imagines the bleeding girl can still hear her when she says she's sorry, so so sorry, to leave her behind.

"I'll save the next," she says. "I promise."

A kiss on the lips and Nova takes flight, her commitment as loud as the guns.

Swan Lake

The night I met her she was wearing all white, as a ruse perhaps, for she was no angel. One look into her eyes and you knew: flammable, ambivalent, relentless.

She was shaped like an angel, though. A tall, lithe frame and pliant limbs. Hair that welcomed light. You could easily imagine wings sprouting from her shoulder blades, powerful wings that would lift her into the air.

She wanted to be a dancer, she said, so I figured she'd be lifted into the air often enough, wings or no wings. Classical ballet, she said, Swan Lake. Her words were born from a dream.

But that was before the steel, grey car soared around the corner and jumped onto the sidewalk where we stood talking, light-headed, not willing to say goodbye. The bar had closed by then. It was a homeless night in late March.

They kept her in the hospital for nearly nine weeks. Whenever I visited, she found her charm in looking bored or attacked the wheels of her chair with a spoon, trying to bend the spokes. Together we made up stories about the devil who hadn't stopped. How he would meet his end, squealing.

On the day she was released, I took her into my arms. I had trained for this. My arms were not wings, but they were strong and skilled. She was wearing all white again on my request. It was a whispering morning in early June.

I took her to the water's edge and lifted her into the air. We waited and watched. On the quiet lake, the swans swam toward us, one by one, eager to meet my dancing love.

CLASSIC

Maya turns thirty-nine today and wants to experience what being a classic woman is all about. Breathe life into the stereotype.

She puts on a full mask of makeup, matches the color of her pumps to her mother's voile scarf from Paris, and practices crying in front of the mirror (in case she's given red roses). She reapplies the makeup.

Unfortunately, her date is late, and having studied her part, Maya knows that in her role as the classic woman, she cannot tolerate waiting, especially not when she has prepared a three-course dinner. By the time poor Felix makes his way over to her house, delayed by golf-club chitchat and Saturday-afternoon traffic and a line at the gas station (*Sorry, no roses*), Maya's resentment is stronger than his flattery. She acts defiantly and pours him stingy glasses of wine.

To make matters worse: Felix is terrible at playing the classic man. She chose him for his age; he's of the previous generation but doesn't act like it. He's too modern for this game, wanting to help her in the kitchen. Does he think the theater of the sexes is a comedy? His weak performance is not helped by his compromised costume: Old butter stains his chinos near his crotch.

As he cuts the chicken, however, his interpretation of the classic man falls less flat, and for the rest of the dinner, Felix properly courts Maya with lines from a male fantasy written decades ago. *You are so sensitive. Other women never get me. This is the best vanilla parfait I've ever tasted.*

When the dialogue peters out, they dance in the living room to Leonard Cohen. Just as Maya's mother would have done today, if she hadn't died of colon cancer weeks before her thirty-ninth birthday.

Felix kisses Maya's neck and strokes her ass. There are no further improvisations before he carries her off to bed. But undressing her, he accidentally knocks over her mother's portrait and the spell is broken.

What's wrong? Felix asks.

It's a valid question. In all fairness, in this scene, the classic man should meet a passionate partner between the sheets. After all the wooing he did. A classic woman may withhold forgiveness long after the man has redeemed himself, yet she will never take revenge during sex. It's not her style. Sex is for union and pleasure, Maya's mother used to say. Not for politics or education. Which may explain why Maya sometimes found her father at the breakfast table long after the divorce.

Still, Maya acts disinterested by Felix's more than adequate erection. In honesty, because she *is* disinterested and no longer willing to play. She gets out of bed, offering no reason, and goes downstairs to finish the wine.

She was only sixteen and still a virgin when her mother died. They never talked about sex, not really. They never compared their experiences or discussed how expectations had changed from one generation to the next. By embodying her mother, Maya had wanted to close that gap.

Liabilities

"Others said no," my son tells me over coffee at my house. "Others stood up for themselves."

Although the trial lies years into the past, nothing makes sense yet. Life went on, naturally. My son couldn't stop life from happening to him, but the self-knowledge he needs to take charge is lacking. Or perhaps it's self-confidence or emotional maturity or existential wit—a devil has swallowed his soul.

He looks like he's been drinking, something stronger than coffee and for a while. His cheeks are inflated. I touch his large hand, not daring to take it into mine until I do. He leaves it there, limp, then offers a squeeze in acknowledgement. I fear his body is acting again, performing a role assigned by someone who isn't him.

How many selves has he betrayed? How many times has he felt himself die?

It started when he was eleven or twelve. A clueless boy. A curious mind. At the time, I worked long days, trying to prove my independence after the divorce. Only in the weekends did I distract myself with the promise of passion. Or the reality of it. There were nights I brought home a woman and found my son in bed wearing his daytime clothes. I never woke him to ask why he hadn't bothered to undress. There were mornings I fried eggs for three and my son refused to eat his share, wouldn't even sit at the table. Because of jealousy, I told myself. Standard teenage behavior.

How often did he evade my eyes or leave my questions unanswered?

For years, I was the mother of a healthy boy who loved judo. So much so, that he went on judo training camps and spent entire afternoons with his black-belted master. Alone.

We drain our cups. I pour more coffee. We each have a life or the pretense of one.

"Other kids said no," my son tells me again, his mind skipping like a record. "Why did I not say no?"

I want to scratch the walls, drag the master pervert from his pen, pummel him with my bare hands until he falls to my feet, bleeding.

Instead, I summon my tenderness and put a trembling palm to my son's inflated cheek. Such a big boy he is now, a man, muscled and unshaven.

The sun breaks through the clouds and floods the room with light. I close my eyes.

I always closed my eyes when I felt my desire sear through my veins. During these rare moments on weekend nights, I lived on my skin and not in my head. I lived in a place of bodily pleasure, blind to a world in which boys fought to forget they had bodies at all.

"Other mothers knew," I tell my son. "Other mothers knew."

If You Think Stars Can't Clap, You're Not Listening

I.

We go out in the predawn cold, when partygoers already went to sleep and delivery people are still in bed. We are architects, constructors of human worlds, but because bureaucrats stamp our work as crime, we do our job in the dark. Like guerillas.

We march together, our footsteps the music to which we sing. A specter is haunting our city—the specter of concrete and asphalt and steel. Trees are razed for car parks, for a falsity called progress.

We declare war on the streets that are as dead and gray as the lives built above their gutters. Homes are like skeletons, dressed in decorations to hide their gloom. Even on the grounds designed for play, we break our bones on stone.

We jostle and laugh in compensation, greet the saplings that survived from last year. Their leaves resemble our souls, aglow with hope for a radiant future.

We hunt traffic islands; they are our favorite game. *Catch this*, we say, as a sack of seeds flies from hand to hand.

We throw and sow, hurl our defiance at the sleeping sun on whom we rely to do its magic. We fertilize matter with our dreams, and we dream of light.

We shout, *Let's go,* when the first morning tram jolts by, and run like cats, disperse. Pride will fill our hearts this spring, for the life that will sway in the wind. If you think stars can't clap, you're not listening.

I slam the door and I'm out, alone and drifting. The streets are deserted, the homes dark. Yet it feels as though behind each window is a clown, laughing at the joke that is me. There's nowhere to go. Nothing to do. One dead end after another. Blind walls. But traffic is picking up now, couching out the toxic fumes of hurry. I'm so sickened by this world and its people, my own wishful thinking. There is no justice, no peace. How do others survive each day from beginning to end and also make it through the night? I walk through my cement city, close my eyes against the dawn. I cannot go on like this. Despair fuels me like black blood.

I turn a corner and freeze. Am I hallucinating? On a usually hideous square, I stand face to face with the sublime—an oasis of color. It's as though I stepped through a secret gate and into a garden. Red poppies peek above the grass, yellow anemones, blue flax, purple snapdragons, a family of daisies. My heart expands in a flood of hope. The flowers are pockets of resistance. All they needed was a touch. I look up at the early morning sun rising over the roofs and let its warm hand rest on my face.

Woman of the Week

WOMAN OF THE WEEK

On Monday, under the weight of routine, she's nothing but sloppy and dull-eyed, like the unhappy housewives you see pushing shopping carts in gray suburbs, even though she's a postal clerk and unmarried and lives downtown.

On Tuesday, she sits down to dinner at a friend's house, pretending to be a Van Gogh potato eater. She gnaws on stale crusts of bread and stabs her fork at the shared platter in front of her, stealing a chunk of duck. She fills each stingy glass up to the brim with the rum she's bought for the host and does so again and again until she feels jolly.

On Wednesday, she wears a drilled face, a face that won't disclose any information unless the owner of the face wants the information to be disclosed. When she isn't blinking and you look at her point blank, you might think she's dead. At night, she watches a talk show and falls asleep with the television blaring.

On Thursday, she wakes up convinced she ought to run a clinic for disturbed adolescents or bury herself in a laboratory until she has isolated a protein that will burn off the stinger of a malarial mosquito like an ignited splinter. All day, she ruminates.

On Friday, after a fruit-only breakfast, she frees herself of the collected sadness so often seen in people who've been dissatisfied since puberty. When she emerges from her home, she looks like a full-souled woman, someone who has only recently abandoned her youth and can easily reach back to reinstall it whenever she wants. At the front desk, she winks and calls her favorite customers by their first names.

On Saturday, she can't conceive of her own death. Fearless, she goes out into the city, looking for trouble and finding none. Her nonchalance is almost spiritual. Wherever she goes, she seems to be at a fabulous party brimming with talk and suspense, even if she only enters the glass doors of the retirement home to pay a visit to her senile mother.

On Sunday, by the lakeshore, her blue eyes are calm with medieval wisdom until dark clouds cluster at the horizon. Standing in the breeze, her long hair sailing, something starved drifts over her. If you ran into her at that moment, you'd see a hunger in her expression that would make you question how satisfied you actually were with your own time on Earth. She wonders, Does responsibility give life meaning?

On Monday, under the weight of routine, she's nothing but sloppy and dull-eyed, like the unhappy housewives you see pushing shopping carts in gray suburbs, even though she's a postal clerk and unmarried and lives downtown.

Snails and Oysters

She loves snails, their soft flavor of slowness. She loves drowning them in olive oil and swallowing them down with raw garlic, a shred of parsley. In between bites, she indulges in sourdough bread toasted black. Flutes of chilled Chablis.

It's essential to her that the man in her bed does not interfere with her love for snails. One complaint about the crumbs, the garlic stench, the grease on pricey sheets, and he's out, banned to the sofa until the last snail has made its sluggish way down her throat.

On the other hand, a man who, despite the size issue, has enough self-confidence to manage a comparison, a hint even, just a meaningful look, well now, that's a man to keep. Her best lover so far watched her eat the snails one by one. Enjoyed seeing the rapture on her face each time the soft flesh caressed her palate. Then called down to the lobby for a plate of oysters.

He slurped and sucked, moaning, putting his tongue right into the shells.

Snails and oysters, he said. They're hermaphrodites. It takes them a long time to figure out which role to play.

They ate in delight, watching each other's mouths. With him she generously shared the chilled Chablis.

DOUBLE LIFE

I felt vulnerable, as anyone would when lying half undressed on a table with their legs spread in metal stirrups and the hands of a stranger touching them, their labia, their cervix—my body.

"Try to relax," the doctor said.

The voice sounded low for a woman's, yet the jaw line was definitely feminine. Fine hair was cropped short and exposed delicate earlobes. Shoulders seemed to be on the broad side.

"Try not to squeeze," the doctor said.

I closed my eyes and only opened them when sun flooded the examination room. Upon my arrival at the healthcare center, it had rained.

The doctor, although frowning in concentration, had an indisputably kind face. The hands touching me felt steady and cool. Competent. And yet I lay there, frustrated and getting angry: I couldn't tell whether the owner of these hands was a man or a woman, and that ambiguity bothered me. It was my right as a vulnerable patient to possess at least that certainty.

"Almost done," the doctor said. "Breathe."

The tag on the unisex uniform showed no first name, as though to confuse me on purpose. I felt ashamed of having that thought, yet that shame didn't stop me from having that thought more than once. The room was heavy with the smell of antiseptic. I didn't know what to expect from this doctor, how to judge their behavior.

When the doctor said "about seven weeks" and changed my pee-stick-based suspicion into an undeniable fact, I felt as though I were falling. Off the green-papered gurney, out of my life.

The doctor looked at me as though to gauge my reaction. I tried to keep my expression neutral, unwilling to be readable, yet I failed. I quickly wiped away my stupid tears. Stupid because incomprehensible, tears from neither joy nor fear.

"Considering your medical history," the doctor said, "I recommend a transvaginal ultrasound to check everything. It will also help me date your pregnancy more accurately." The doctor waited for my response, then added: "It's completely safe."

From the cracked window came the shouts of children playing. Boys and girls who raised their voices to assert their existence.

"Will an ultrasound reveal … the gender?"

The doctor smiled—in a mocking way? "No. At this stage of gestation, we cannot see the gender, but the procedure will show us a heartbeat."

I nodded and agreed to go ahead. There was something beautiful about watching sound.

As the doctor inserted a probe into my uterus and observed my insides on the screen, I observed the doctor. They could be a transgender person in transition. Or an androgynous person who liked the status quo. Or someone who was largely unaware of the doubt their appearance caused in others. There were no family pictures on the wall.

I fought it as much as I could, but the doctor's competent hands began to feel cool with indifference.

"This is the gestational sac"—the doctor pointed at the screen—"and this is the yolk sac."

Really? To me it was all blurry vagueness. Clouds once again obscured the sun.

I considered asking the doctor how they identified, but I didn't want to embarrass myself and be on the wrong side of things. I didn't want to be rude. Bringing up a person's gender is like pointing out a flaw: *You're not clear enough; you're leading a double life.* Then again, if the mixed signals were intentional, meant to destabilize a vulnerable patient like me, I had the right to object.

"That's all," the doctor said. "You may get dressed."

I pulled up my slacks in rage. I wanted my life to be easier. I wanted to know how to correctly refer to my doctor. I wanted to understand my missing response to what was growing inside of me. Pregnant women ought to be happy or horrified. Not indecisive. Not something in between.

Fully dressed again, I sat down in front of the desk. The doctor was talking to me, but I had trouble listening, and when the flow of words stopped, I asked only one question. "Is everything okay?"

"Yes. You and the fetus are healthy."

I cried, immensely grateful for the doctor's choice of words, for the neutrality I had previously mis-imagined as indifference. I wasn't ready for anyone to tell me that my "baby" was doing fine.

It seemed almost logical now that I had no clear feelings about becoming a mother—there was no child yet, no boy or girl or they. There was only potential, the possibility for growth.

On the way out, the doctor handed me a brochure about additional screening tests and options for unplanned pregnancies—another lesson in nonjudgmental behavior.

The rain was falling again, and as I waited in the hall for it to cease, I smiled through my tears. The weather made me think of my grandmother and the Breton expression: *Il fait beau plusieurs fois par jour*. The weather is good multiple times a day.

Repairs

What if she'd talked to the two indigenous women on the day she first heard rumors about the storm? An opening is easy to make, a smile followed by a few kind words. They appeared so at ease with each other in their embroidered dresses, strolling along the shore. Soft-faced, shiny-eyed, full of attention. They pulled at her like the tide yet she resisted. She could have asked their advice about what to do if the storm hit their coast, could have joined them on their walk, the sky still so warm and blue, manta rays jumping from the waves with a spray and catching the sun like living rainbows.

What if the women had invited her to stay with them in case the storm became dangerous? Unlike her, they probably lived in a stone house and not an ill-chosen holiday cabana that was bound to lose its palm-thatched roof in the first furious gust. Had she been less shy, had she made that easy opening, she would now not face the unforgiving walls of her dark apartment. She would stand on the beach instead, clearing debris and breathing clean air. She and the wise women would have braved the storm together.

What if, however, the women had not come true on their promise, had made an excuse to turn her down in the end? People are rarely as a kind as they seem, and her uselessness would have escaped from her skin like a bad smell. She would have made no exit strategy, no alternative plans. She would have found herself abandoned and without protection in a Category 3 hurricane, unable to hide in a tree stump like the cat-sized iguana who visited her for breakfast each day. The wind would have dragged her white ass from the cabana and smashed her against the agaves. Or the rain would have liquefied her hill, which was never hers, and she would have mud-slid down into the ocean's hungry mouth.

Nonsense. She could have taken refuge in a stone church, a government shelter. Any reasonable soul would have hosted her in times of need. Life after the storm might have been unpleasant for a while, no running water or electricity or privacy, but she would have been present for the repairs. Cultural divides are easier to bridge when you work toward a common goal. Instead of being a spoiled tourist, a pity case, swallowing self-reproach with each chili shrimp, she would have been a promise, a foreigner who had not chickened out.

What if she had met these soft-faced women again in the village after the storm? She might have lent them a hand lifting their bamboo fence, offered to pay for tools and materials. They might have taught her how to fix a table or cook Oaxacan tamales. She might not have been able to make a difference in their lives, but they would have made a difference in hers. She might have finally felt part of the world.

Battle of Brushes

When we passed the antique shop for the second time that week, there was another painting of a Dutch windmill in the window, substandard as usual.

"Don't be mad at me for asking."

Although Albert didn't talk anymore, these were his words. The appeal in his eyes shone clear as day.

I took it stoically. Having been dragged inside the shop again and again during the past year, I'd gotten used to buying him sloppy art.

The place was deserted, except for the knickknacks and the owner and us. I chatted with Ellen as though I didn't suspect her of baiting Albert. He couldn't resist a windmill—one of his addled obsessions—and being his wife, I couldn't resist Albert. The paintings were a tax on our retirement, but something in me always gave way. I had taken to wearing thicker sweaters indoors to save on gas.

Ellen bubble-wrapped the package, her face the incarnation of gloating. Where did she keep finding these windmills? Perhaps it was some type of witchcraft. Her shop always smelled smoky and sweet as if she were cooking up tricks disguised as treats. A specialty for the elderly.

While I handed her the money, I noticed a blue paint stain on her desk, a stain that hadn't been there the other day when Albert and I had bought another windmill. The blue corresponded with the blue of sky that took up most of the painting that Albert now pressed to his chest. The work suddenly looked even more amateur and hastily made. I wasn't surprised—I'm a seasoned cynic and almost envied Ellen's shamelessness—but my mind perceived a challenge. When confronting a hungry wolf, guile is your only weapon.

"Do you have an easel for sale?" I asked.

Ellen didn't think my question was funny. She looked like a pine tree that's been struck by lightning yet still has its needles.

Outside, all was quaint, and Albert and I made one last stop to get supplies before going home. For the rest of the day, life was as simple as looking at Albert's face, nearly transparent, beauty flowing from his brow. He painted one windmill after another, each as familiar as my dreams, until there was nothing left of light.

Floris, Fate, and the Friendly Stranger

Ella buys the boy a burger, ruffles his hair, bounces his body on her knees. Time has jumped back and she can do this again, the sky high and wide.

The boy cries for his mother in a toy store, scared by the robots that talk to him. Ella soothes him with promises of reunion, a cherry ice cream cone. At the curl of his smile, their joint future shines.

Does he remember what happened to his mother at the grocery's checkout? It all went so fast. The screams and sirens. The mother's exit on a gurney. It's not kidnapping when medics deliver a child into your open arms. Did they believe she was his aunt? Ella promised to keep him safe.

The boy cries again on a crosswalk; her grip on his hand is too tight. He doesn't like it when she calls him Quinn, when she shows him the street where the car knocked them down. One step in the wrong direction, she says, and you're outside your life.

At dusk, the boy whining and tired, they pass through the hospital's revolving doors. If his mother has survived the stroke, Ella will do the right thing. If not, Quinn's room is waiting, unchanged. They will learn to love each other again. He'll grow back into his clothes.

The hospital lights are relentlessly bright; the reception, busy. Would they let her keep the boy if she asks? Never. Real aunts or grandmothers will stand in the way. Endless adoption waiting lists. For her and the boy fate should decide.

LOST AND FOUND

My younger brother and I took turns watching the little boat through the binoculars. The boat was a rubber inflatable loaded with passengers waving and calling. For help, it seemed.

Our widowed father, who took us sailing on his yacht on the Mediterranean each year, stood on deck reefing his jib and didn't notice a thing. The rubber boat to our starboard was almost too small to be spotted with the naked eye.

The wind became more furious by the minute.

"Should we tell Dad?" I asked my brother.

"Pirates leave no witnesses when they steal a ship," was his reply.

I thrusted the helm into his hands and peered once more through the binoculars. The travelers were signaling wildly and looked untrustworthy. Was it really a ruse?

The menacing clouds on the horizon got even darker and our father said, "That doesn't look good." He meant the unexpected storm.

He retook the helm from us and turned his yacht around, back to the coast, sails flapping like wounded wings. I switched on the engine for extra speed and forgot about the possible pirates when forty-knot winds whipped the water into foam.

Waves rose to enormous heights. We held on tight as the storm built to its dark intensity.

We reached the harbor after the downpour broke. With eyes burning and hands wrinkled, we moored our ship as best as we could. The night delivered furious gusts and thunderclaps, an inconsolable sky.

In the morning the storm had passed. My brother and I went to comb the beach; the sea often spits up treasures. But the path was blocked by orange tape. There had been an accident, a police officer explained. A boat with refugees had capsized. Their bodies had washed up on shore.

"Such tragic misfortune," she said. "All these pleasure boats out yesterday and nobody saw these people in time to pick them up."

I met my brother's eyes.

"It's a cruel world," he said.

I insisted we would never tell our father.

Saving Lives Left and Right

"What's the point of it all?" he asked. "Green hair, deafening music, drugs that make your teeth fall out. It's unnerving. Immature."

"You're conservative," I said.

Matthew, the curious world traveler, the Republican-bred Democrat, shook his head in defiance, taking offense. We were on our third beer and our first date, which wasn't technically a date, because we'd met just hours before—with humps on our backs, our feet malformed in fins—and had no need to set a date: We were already together.

"There are two types of alternatives," he said, meaning *alternative people*. "One type thinks that behaving out-of-whack makes them look like a genius. The other type is too mentally unstable to act normal."

The stakes were raised. "Define 'normal'."

Matthew was my diving instructor. In his tight rubber suit he'd looked like a package I wanted to unwrap.

"Let me give you an example," he said. "I was on a job once, salvaging a wreck in the Aegean Sea. After a day of hard and honest work I meet this dude. We're moored to the dock—on Sifnos this is, or no, Kimolos, yes, Greece's viper island, although I only saw one miserable snake. I'm on deck packing up gear, and this guy comes up to the boat, long Rasta hair, tanned through, purple wrap around his hips. 'How much to fill up my tanks?' he asks."

I raised my hand as though in school, which was supposed to be ironic. I meant to show him how he was speaking in excess, behaving like a teacher instead of a date. Some men improve their behavior when you make them aware of what repels you. But the irony was lost on Matthew. He paused and gestured at me as though I'd needed his permission to interrupt.

"How did you know he was a Rastafarian?" I asked.

"What do you mean?"

"You said 'Rasta hair.' Did you discuss his beliefs?"

"Fine, let's call him a hippie. I ask for his diving license, which is the *normal* thing to do. We had a compressor on deck, you see, and sometimes we filled up the locals. Free of charge."

"How generous."

He studied me, confused. It amazes me how men these days can still be unaccustomed to female sarcasm.

"*Normally* these locals show me their license," Matthew went on, "but this guy only glares at me and walks off."

"Maybe he went home to get it?"

He shook his head, his clean-shaven, well-groomed, earnest-faced head. "No. I know the type. These kinds of people think they're above the law. Rules don't apply to them. As he's walking off, I call out to him. 'Hey, the sea is dangerous, man,' I say, 'I might be saving your life.' It was *meltemi* season, you know."

"What's that?"

Oh, Matthew loved me again. My interest had thickened into a real question and now he could legitimately explain things to me.

"Strong winds, rough currents," he said. "Anyway, that night I go out for a drink with a buddy. A local ouzo bar. And guess what?"

"The outlaw is there."

He grasped my wrist. Heat shot up my arm. "Worse! The guy owns it, the bar. Runs it with his friends."

"His Rasta hippie friends."

"Right. And there are all sorts of ancient coins on the walls and other sea trophies. I figure: They're treasure hunters, illegal bounty divers, stealing artifacts that belong in museums. My instincts were right from the start. Rules don't apply to them. Still, I try to be nice, you know, for the island's sake, but the guy refuses to serve me. Can you believe that? 'Alcohol is dangerous, man,' the dude says, 'I might be saving your life.'"

I laughed out loud, really loud, thinking it was a joke on Matthew's part. I like people who can comfortably self-deprecate. But Matthew released my wrist and leaned back, as if more offended by me than by the dude.

I drained my beer. I figured we would not be unwrapping each other tonight, but I wasn't sorry. I was probably saving my own life.

Ugly Thing

I'm taking the kitchen table, because you don't remember how we hauled it together in sweating harmony from the Queen's Day secondhand market through the celebrating streets to our first home. We ate raw herring that night proudly seated around its oak on compact book boxes stacked so high our feet dangled. I'm also taking the books, no doubt about that—the hours we spent in each other's company yet in separate worlds add up to a decade I'm keen to preserve. We fought over the Moroccan rug more bitterly than any rug warrants, and you won, paid the perfumed hawker, so here I am rolling it up for me to take. If you knew what I was doing, you would object.

I walk through the house, tagging the objects that mark our growth, the couch for Sunday mornings, me sandwiched between animal leather and human tongue, the letterbox in which you placed the amulet from your college friend next to my brother's harmonica. We used to speak the same language. Breathed the same air when I bled far too much after six months. What I cannot take is the spot in front of the sink where you stood as I spied on you plucking your eyebrows. There was so much I wanted from you and so little I dared to ask for.

You're not clear about what you want to keep, so I'm making all the decisions. I won't take the clock I used to stare at when you failed to show up and I waited, waited. Won't take the throw you slept under when I banned you from the bed. I didn't know how much I was hiding and couldn't guess how little you understood. I thought we still had time to learn. But we were mostly together, though, weren't we? Even if not always in harmony.

I'm done with tagging the past. My future without you is somewhere beyond that door. I don't know who of us got the better deal in the end. Your heart ached for a while, yet you seem to have forgotten your unhappiness. Is it easier to be content when the present is all you have? I help you get up from the chair that I'm not taking, that I'll gladly destroy with an axe—you would have hated such an ugly thing had you still been yourself. You lean on me as we walk through the front door. We still exist, I suppose, yet not as who we were when we hauled that kitchen table home or fought over the Moroccan rug. I'm taking your arm, yet I'm leaving you behind.

THE HARDEST THING

The hardest thing about camping is not the getting lost on the way or the fighting over who was in charge of map reading. You've been together long enough to know how to counter road rage with a cornucopia of candy bars and loud music. Eventually, you arrive at your destination anyway.

The hardest thing is not the setting up camp. Tired from driving all day, you unload the car together and carry everything uphill to that unbeatable-view location, not complaining about how it's already dark and the view invisible. You're shocked by the mountain's deep cold and build a fire immediately, hoping that the flames will warm your bones through the tent's non-insulating fabric. Fire may also scare the bears, or at least fade your fear.

The hardest thing is not the earth, although it's like stone and backbreaking. During meals outdoors, you crush sand between your teeth because of the pole wind blowing into your bowl. You foresee that the blisters from hammering stakes into the ground will freeze into calluses. Even the light is unyielding. But to be frank, you toughen up nicely and soon learn how to brace yourself against the world.

The hardest thing about camping, you think, is the no-phone-signal intimacy of the long evenings inside the tent. It gets dark rather early this season and you're not at that age yet when you can go to sleep at ten. So there you are, all wired up with the frustrations of the day, and no escape, nothing to do but sit there and look your loved one in the eye. You talk about past adventures and future dreams. Make confessions. Console each other. You glimpse pieces of the other you thought had died.

But I'm not telling this right. Because the hardest thing, really, is not the intimacy itself, especially not once it's established and undeniable. The hardest thing is the knowledge that everything—the winding roads, the beautiful cold, the heartening fire, the vital reconnection—will be gone the moment you break up camp and go home. You try to be blind to this looming end and stay in the moment. You try to forget about the daily dose of disappointment waiting for you upon your return. With all your might you try to deny the truth that the hardest thing about camping is the realization that home is not the place where your life happens.

Woman of the Year

WOMAN OF THE YEAR

In January, a missing creeps into her life like the winter cold. She still enjoys her days, climbing mountains, sorting books, firing kick-ass emails to clients. And she isn't lonely: Friends speak to her from screens and across from tables whenever she reaches out. But there's a nameless absence that feels like a deprivation, as though she lost something along the way.

In February, he smiles at her from afar, from the health food aisle in the supermarket, a distance she must travel. Immediately, she's alert, aroused. Traveling excites her. Who will be the first to advance? She denies it with her heart, her mind, her feminist truths, but once he pours her a glass of pinot noir in the café next door, she wonders whether what she's been missing in her life could be a man.

In March, she feels whimsical, lost in the complicated world of sex. She seems to have returned to that experimental stage of youth in which one wants to try out everything. Her energy is startling. If only she could channel some of her libido into her career.

In April, they glance up from the present to peer into the future and compare notes. They zoom in on overlaps that promise bonding: exotic destinations, no children, art exhibitions, the intention to stay kind to the world no matter what. We found each other at the perfect moment, he tells her. She nods, although she doesn't agree. She has the feeling of being found, not of having found, and secretly ponders the difference.

In May, she casually takes a weekend off from being together. He responds with neediness. Having grown up with three sisters, he believes he bears the key to any female psyche, and what her behavior signifies, clearly, is that she's holding back. I am? she asks. Yes, he replies, you're afraid of losing your independence. Should we smother each other instead? she asks. Yes, oh, yes, please! They make love there and then as though needing to convince an invisible audience of their undying devotion.

In June, he tells her she's too physical for him, which makes her feel vulgar, temporarily, and confused. But perhaps he's right; who is she to tell him what he likes? She will have to masturbate when he's not around, even if that means she must take her habits into the tiled confines of his hallway bathroom.

In July, his complaints multiply. She is too aloof, too busy, too defensive, not committed enough, not sufficiently interested in his dreams. It appears he has fallen in love with an improved version of her, an ideal non-existing twin she can only emulate in short bursts. But she's trying, genuinely trying, and that should count for something, they both believe, even if she often fails to get it right.

In August, she travels with her widowed mother on a cruise from Trieste to Siracusa, ignoring most yet not all Italian men. Reckoning with the fragility of his male ego, she only sends him pictures of architectural marvels and gustatory delights. The cream-leaking hand-sized cannola breaks him nonetheless. She is passive-aggressively unmanning him long distance.

In September, she tries a new strategy. Whenever she doesn't understand what she has done wrong, or not done right, she apologizes anyway, and smiles as he praises her for having seen the light. Their lovemaking, however, sinks to the level of nostalgia. They do it for old time's sake. She imagines what it might feel like to be him, to be so sure you haven't done anything wrong.

In October, she brings an end to the make-believe and lets an unfamiliar meanness inspire her deeds. If you must know the truth, she says, I'm always late because you're just too boring to be with for long. After having feared to displease him by accident, it comes as a freedom to displease him deliberately. Now his hard eyes and cold shoulders are at least deserved.

In November, she feels so rejected that she suggests they break up. He interprets her suggestion as the definitive proof that he has been right all along and she never truly loved him. When she doesn't contradict him, taking the easy way out, he turns her suggestion into a fact that hinges on a dare: They will separate unless she sacrifices her independence.

In December, she feasts on theater and apple pie without regrets. The vague missing of the previous winter has morphed into an existential puzzle that she may never solve. But a puzzle isn't a problem. To live is to wonder every day.

men. [illegible] with [illegible] fragility of the [illegible] the only [illegible] pictures of architectural marvels and [illegible] delights. The [illegible]-looking [illegible] him nonetheless. She [illegible] distance.

In September, she [illegible] humors and [illegible] not [illegible] he [illegible] the light [illegible] however, [illegible]

[illegible]

[illegible] independent.

In December, the [illegible] in theater and apple pie [illegible] of the previous winter has [illegible] puzzle that one may never solve. But [illegible] not a problem. To live is to wonder every day.

FIVE FORBIDDEN FRIENDS

The gifts lie carefully wrapped and labeled on the glass side table like museum items on display. Anabel will receive my emerald ring; with her trust-me face, she extracted the true story from me of how my grandmother swallowed that ring in a jewelry store and used it, cleaned of shit, to purchase a boat ticket and escape the war. Lexi, my book club pal, will get my mom's fake pharmacy diploma, and her perfectionist's eyes will spot the spelling mistake my mom's employers missed. For Femke, I packed the blond wig that she'd spied on my head when we ran into each other unexpectedly near the gym where we usually hung out and that had made her suspicious of me for a while; it might soothe her anxiety to know she wasn't paranoid after all. Kes will delight in the secret pockets of my long leather coat to smuggle illegal snacks into the art cinema where we first met. And Malou will own the calligraphy pen I used to practice my signatures; she runs the health food store where I buy my raw cacao, and with her sixth chakra so beautifully balanced, she will feel what I've been up to just by holding the Lamy in her hand.

My five forbidden friends wander into my home like stray animals and hesitantly accept a cocktail that swirls toxic green. Trust me, I say, it's not too strong. They appear nervous yet curious, willing to be seduced by whatever I have planned. They've known their version of me for nearly two years, which is a long time in my book, and they smelled smoke when I invited them to this get-together. I've never been at your place before, they said. You hate dinner parties. What's the special occasion? You can't even cook!

I clock each of them stealing glances at the table, but none dare to examine the gifts up close. Politeness imposes patience. I imagine their faces as they tear off the ribbons, wide-eyed or frowning, perhaps a knowing smile. It occurs to me only now that I risk hurting them by exposing what I hid before. But in their place, I would feel touched for having received a clue, an insight—wouldn't they? After all, our connections are real.

I serve bowls of tofu curry over steaming white rice because I once made the mistake of telling Kes I was a vegetarian to avoid eating at the hamburger joint where they might have recognized me, and I let Anabel, my hairdresser, believe I was gluten-intolerant to bypass the bakery where they have yet to discover my creative bookkeeping. These little lies have haunted me more than the scams that made them necessary. I don't lie to friends—it's not who I am. And if I lie by omission, it's only to keep them safe. Friends can't be liable when left in the dark.

We talk about men and their tricks, about electrical company bastards and bosses who stink. After we've ferried all the dirty dishes to the kitchen sink like an oiled team, I distribute my gifts. Just a token of gratitude for coming here tonight, I say, for being my friend. I ask them to not open their gifts until they're home, and my confidence that they will observe my request makes me weepy for the first time that night.

At the door, I hold my goodbyes in my heart, so they won't see it in my fleeing eyes, sense it in my exaggerated hug, hear it in my loaded voice. I feel split and appear intact like on any other day. When I later lift my luggage into the car and drive off, I wonder whether they will come together one day, perhaps for the first anniversary of my disappearance. Will they bring what I gave them and put the pieces together? Will they see me whole and know me better than I'll ever know myself?

they pray, and my confidence that they will observe my [illegible] me the way for the [illegible] that night.

As the [illegible] goodbyes in my heart, [illegible] seen [illegible] among [illegible] passengers [illegible] my landed [illegible] like an [illegible] When I later [illegible] and I wonder [illegible] together [illegible] for the [illegible] With [illegible] together [illegible] I [illegible]

An Interesting Case

In the matter of doctors, I prefer the ones who are young. They're still interested in your body. When you put your ailments on display, they act as though you're handing them a scientific article stuffed with fascinating, mind-blowing facts. Some people wouldn't dream of surrendering themselves into the care of great inexperience. A doctor's face without wrinkles gives them the creeps. Not me.

Once, I suffered a skin condition that wouldn't let up after fighting it with the usual armory of moisturizers, cortisone creams, salt-water baths, dry brushing, soda soaking, oils, ointments, cold compresses, disinfecting sprays, and long hours staring in awe. I went to see a dermatologist in Paris. He was an older man. As he listened to my complaints concerning my mysterious affliction, he worked hard at giving me the impression he had seen every possible human skin disease imaginable at least a thousand times. From across his desk, he glanced at the red patches on my lower arms and suggested he should test me for perfume and metal allergies. As if I hadn't heard that one before. I was as bored listening to him as he was looking at me. So I got up and left.

I don't like doctors all that much, generally speaking. And particularly speaking, I dislike the ones who are patronizing or uncurious. For years, I avoided doctors completely for that reason until I developed a peeling condition and went to see a podiatrist in Florence. She was a young woman. She had just graduated from whatever program you go through before they let you touch anyone real and alive. When I showed her my heels, she pushed her glasses all the way up her nose, which heartened me. She also turned on the spotlight above the white papered gurney on which she had asked me to lie down. Afterwards, she bombarded me with questions that I couldn't answer without telling her the truth.

But that old dermatologist in Paris? Not a single question. If he had asked about my habits, my likes and dislikes, my own suspicions, if he had been as curious as his younger colleague in Florence, he might have learned that I used crushed chili peppers to create these beautiful patches on my skin, not perfume or metals. Older doctors are not easily shocked, so you can be more truthful with them. The problem is that I am lost in their eyes, whereas in the eyes of a young doctor, I am an interesting case to be solved.

UNDESERVED GIFT

Nina won nothing in the lottery of birth. Her parents are selfish, her hands incompetent, and her rights to happiness appear permanently stalled. Friends have come and gone like tides, leaving envy in their wake. She lacks what she needs to free her life from the prison it has become. Does she have no destiny? Perhaps it's time for a dose of consolatory self-care in the Asian sun.

Nina tours the noisy streets in anger, disgusted by the hustlers, the stink of feet. Trash and neon everywhere. Beggars like hungry ghosts. Where is her postcard paradise? She scrimped for years, tracked rates for months, and traveled for days. Only to land in this heinous hot hole of hell. No one warned her about the thieves on mopeds. The euphemisms on "Massage Parlor" menus. The city air is so impure, she can't even breathe.

A girl grabs Nina's hand. Ten years old, eleven maybe, sunken eyes uplifted. Her saffron shirt is dirty and hangs off her scarred shoulder like a rag. *Please, I have sick mother.* Nina jerks free, afraid of touch and sickness. Yet she didn't mean to startle the girl. *I'm sorry. I have no cash.* Which is a lie. She's just too stupid for not having loose change and too smart to open her wallet on the street.

Nina returns to the hotel. Sunglasses on despite the dusk, protecting her eyes from the stares and grime. In her damp room, the sheets itch and the mosquitos buzz inside the netting. She lies in the dark with her eyes open, resenting her choices and the world. Her unhappiness shames her like a crime.

Car horns blast and drunkards holler. But from the noise uncoils the sound of music. A melody lassoes into the room through the open window and hooks her, pulling her from the bed. It's as though she's hearing her name.

Nina leans out the window. Below in the dirt stands another girl, dressed in hunger and pain. Scraggy fingers plucking sitar strings, playing music to honor the night. It's an exquisite song, notes unfurling—an undeserved gift.

A man appears and the girl stops playing. He speaks to her gruffly, takes her by the elbow, forces her into a doorway, muffles her mouth with his. *No!* The sitar falls to the ground—a dull plunk. Nina can almost feel the brutal hand between her thighs, the cruelty of ringed fingers.

Hatred as sharp as a knife cuts through her. She shouts down, *Leave her alone!* The man gazes up, looks for the woman who dares to disturb him, and she shouts, *I see you*!

He lets the girl go, stumbles back, and rushes off into the dark. The girl picks up her sitar before turning to the window and meeting Nina's eyes. *I see you*, Nina says again yet in a different tone. *I see you.*

THE MIND READER

I am a woman of discipline, which is to say: I don't act at random. But I once slept with a mind reader on a whim.

I failed to recognize his abilities in the Van Gogh Museum, where we met on one of its special events. We exchanged small talk followed by flirtatious remarks disguised as small talk. He could have easily been the most unattractive man I had ever been talking to, but I get nervous when men flirt with me and when nervous I get polite, which is often interpreted by these men as flirtatiousness on my part.

Anyway, we talked, and as we talked I noticed how this man was able to read my mind. Each time I bit my tongue and swallowed my words, he would voice what I was unwilling to share with him. Such as: God, you stink. Or: What type of idiot are you? I consistently denied that these were my thoughts and tried to remain calm by drinking a lot of cheap wine, which did no good.

After a while, the mind reader told me that he did not resent me for having such low thoughts of him and actually liked me for not being able to express them. Next thing I knew, I slept with him. He was thirty years my senior and twice my weight. He dressed ghastly, harbored terrible political ideas, and was probably someone who let his mother iron his shirts, but I slept with him regardless. He kept hearing my mind say how he appalled me, and the only way to prove him wrong, was to confuse him with sex. Everyone knows that sex is by far the best way to confuse a man.

When he rolled off me and started to pull on his corduroys, jerking them over his sagging ass, he said that many women had fucked him out of pity, but that he had never met anyone before to whom the privacy of her head meant more than the intrusion of her body.

GUILLOTINE

I

Geert offers his fantasy as a gift, an early Christmas present.

"There's no need for you to be so timid," he says, squeezing her left breast.

Her objections to his "gift" go unheard. Perhaps they aren't loud enough. Or he disregards them as modesty. Evening muteness takes over and they watch TV in an atmosphere of forced tolerance.

A week later, he gives her a time and place, and she is annoyed. Unwilling.

"But we talked about this," he says. His annoyance is stronger.

Before long, she gives up, gives in, gives. Because he has already paid the guy—of course it's a guy. Because she doesn't want to be a spoilsport and supply Geert with ammunition. Their life together is degenerating—one thing they agree on—yet they have seven months left on their one-year lease, so moving out now would mean a financial disaster.

II

The atelier on Prinsengracht is impressive. Designer furniture, antique ladders, a stash of theatrical costumes, masks, and props.

She has arrived unprepared, physically, mentally. The photographer tells her to brush her wind-blown hair and hide her clothes behind the paper screen.

"Excuse me?"

"Yes, I'm shooting you naked," he says, as though it's the most natural thing in the world.

She considers walking out. You forgot to mention the details, she would tell Geert. And he would reply that she must have misunderstood. As always, there would be no recording to play back. His word against hers. The fight would win.

While she undresses, she talks herself into the idea, like she talked herself into cohabitation. She hates to admit that she's in this Geert-mess because of a pathetic infatuation. She was impulsive, hopeful, blind.

Her socks and underwear leave her with seam-indented flesh. The photographer can probably smell her embarrassment the moment she appears from behind the paper screen.

"Don't worry," he says, setting up his camera. "There's post-production."

He doesn't seem to notice her much during the shoot, which is reassuring. As though he's looking at an object instead of a person. He must have done this a million times.

"Please lift your thigh off the floor. Perfect. Please raise your chin. Thank you."

She complies as best as she can until he tells her that she's free to go.

His last words echo on her way back to that place she can no longer call home.

III

A selection of twenty digital photographs arrives in Geert's inbox. *Her* body in *his* inbox, because *he* paid for the session.

Their favorite shot will be blown-up, printed, and framed. It's included in the price.

The idea of her naked self as a life-size image on the wall depresses her. But complaining about the arrangement now seems silly. She should have asked the right questions in advance. Her mistake.

Together they sit on the sofa, laptop on his lap. The photos are attractive, which doesn't surprise her. Her body is young, well made, and the photographer was professional. But will any of these pictures improve their sex life? She assumes this was Geert's goal—as though sex would fix them.

"Fantastic," he says, clicking through the results. "You must be thrilled."

He doesn't realize that she's done him a favor. It's infuriating.

They compare how her breasts hang or poke on each shot.

She thinks of rental rates in Amsterdam and their unaffordable heights.

"But my smile is so lame," she says, commenting on the photo he calls his favorite.

"Who cares?"

She gets up, wondering if they've ever spoken the same language. "You choose."

When she sees his grin of dark pleasure, she regrets her surrender. He loves winning. With each sick victory, he's gnawing away at her autonomy.

On a dead December day, she returns from work and finds a large, framed photograph hanging on their living room wall. He stands beside it, proud, a bandage on his finger where he must have hammered himself instead of the nail.

A noose seems to tighten around her neck. The lighting and composition are flattering in this shot. The photographer has matched her curves to the background curtains. Even the airbrushing is smart, leaving her cute moles and dimples intact. But she doesn't recognize herself. She sees an anonymous body. Not even a woman. A body.

"Why's my head missing?"

He reacts as though her question is an offense. "I asked for it."

"Asked for what?"

"To have the picture cropped."

A surge of humiliation is followed by a rage so strong, it makes her calm as ice.

"Why?"

"Because ... you're naked. And we have friends coming over all the time. I thought it would make you uncomfortable. Hanging there. Naked."

How considerate. "So why *do* I hang there naked?"

She might as well have suggested they'd fuck—he couldn't be more baffled. "But nobody will suspect it's you! I made you unrecognizable."

"You chopped off my head."

He throws up his arms as if warding away an evil spirit. "Give me a break. You always make me into a monster. Why give it such an awful spin? You're gorgeous. I made you look gorgeous."

Silence drifts into the room like poisonous gas. She checks the horizon for the arrival of dawn, but his face remains dark.

"Why did you want this photo of me?" she asks.

"You don't like it?"

"That's not the point."

"I wanted you to know how beautiful you are," he says, softening, perhaps thinking he's getting a chance to make things right. "Look. Will you please look? This is how I see you."

She looks. She sees a body. No head. "I feared as much."

Outside, the streets are wet and slick as though it has been raining for years. She walks into an uncertain future with her most important possessions on her back. She should have plotted her exit better, but didn't her aunt say that her renter was soon returning to Brazil? In the meantime, there are sofas friends have offered to her in the past. Victory fires her steps. She's free to come and go.

CLOSED CIRCLE

The others and I hike up the winding trail from the riverbank to Dettifoss, queen of glacial waterfalls. The canyon is steep and stark as though warning me for what's to come. Forty-five meters high, a hundred meters wide, two hundred cubic meters of water per second. This Icelandic queen draws tourists from around the world like magic.

I feel alone at first, not part of the group, but I soon find myself having an okay time, mingling with the others, sharing in the happy anticipation of all. Do thoughts adapt and intertwine when you talk inside clouds of vapor? While my new colleagues and I compare notes on growing up, relationships, the contrast between pushers and pullers, the revolutionary potential of art, it's as though the distance between us gets smaller and our boundaries less fixed.

We hear the royal fall long before we see her and when we do see her, beyond the line of rocks, we drop into silence and stare in awe.

This is what we've come to experience, a beauty so great it pauses the self.

The closer we get to the fall, the more we feel her raw power, the fury in the drop. The ground trembles beneath our feet and the roar fills our heads.

We scramble toward the gorge. Gushing folds of water ripple and splash, hurling themselves down in a cascading flow. You are flesh, says the queen. You are perishable.

We each get as close as we dare, which means we break apart. There are those who carefully stand back and those who feel called to live dangerously.

There are no guard rails to keep us from the edge. Just a sign shrouded in vapor, easy to ignore.

Three of us lean out over the roar and stare down, holding on to a stunted tree. Spray from the depth whirls up into a gorgeous mist kissing my face.

I imagine my body diving down with the water, merging with its force and speed, the pull of the currents, the life slipping and rushing over me, and my whole self being swallowed up into the white foam, unbound, changing, crashing onto the stones of the riverbed.

I gauge the two others with whom I share the edge. Do they fear or long?

Be honest, do you ever dream of letting go? I ask.

The others seem disturbed by my question and exchange looks with each other. One of them answers me with, Do you?

Come on, I say, let's get even closer.

The others withdraw, their bodies no longer leaning out.

Once again, I am alone. But alone can be good. Alone is benign.

I let go of the stunted tree and inch forward.

The others call out to me, call me back, fling their voices over the royal crash. They might as well scream, *What's wrong with you?*

I face the void, peering into the fall where every sparkle of light discloses more darkness.

Down there I would be free, part of something real. No pretending. No trying. Just falling for eternity, like in a closed circle.

I look up, uncertain about what to do, and face the others. Their expression appears strangely familiar to me, as though fear and longing are the same in the end.

A sweet intoxication sweeps through me when hands that cannot touch me reach out to me nonetheless. We hold one another's gaze until all of us are back in the safety zone, admiring the queen from afar.

[illegible] I would be [illegible], part of something real. No [illegible] just falling for eternity, like in a closed [illegible]

[illegible] and face the others. Their [illegible] appears strangely familiar to me, as though [illegible] in the curl.

[illegible] sweeps through [illegible] that [illegible] to the [illegible] We [illegible] [illegible]

Attic

My silent mother returns to our silent home with stitches in her brow, swollen cheeks, her warmth spent. I've barely slept since they took her away and sleep even less now. Each morning, I dab her wounds and brush her skin with my lips, crushed to find her scent is gone.

We don't talk about the boys. We don't mention how they doubled our days, promised us purpose, helped us hope. We don't dare to wonder where they are now. They were foreigners and strangers, yet also ours. Their absence rattles our bones.

Force must have been used from the start, cracking my mother on the third day. What happened afterward, I wonder, when they returned to our house, went straight to the attic, busted the secret door, and didn't find what they'd been promised?

I tell myself, had I not told the boys to run, all her suffering would have been in vain.

At night, I relive the moment right before they dragged her away, when my eyes told her unambiguously that I would never forgive her if she betrayed the boys.

I make new soaps and experiment with the recipe—more herbs, less sunflower oil—not knowing what I hope to accomplish.

Time passes and my mother's wounds heal. Even her warmth flares up: She strokes my cheek and says, I would have survived the moment, not the memory. But my mother's words don't help. The world in which I am innocent and brave seems no more real than the world in which I can fly.

She used to smell so reassuringly, woody and wondrous, like a poem in summer rain. I wish it were my nose, my guilt embodied, and she has returned unchanged.

INNER THIEF

Her husband says they have enough for the two of them. He folds his hand over hers, the one wielding the knife, and she stops slicing the breakfast bread. Their eyes meet. The word "enough" sounds foreign to her, as though it has lost all meaning. They eat one lightly buttered sandwich each and drink substitute coffee.

All day long, the ghost of his hollow word haunts her around the store. Her husband is a grocer and she works, unpaid, as his clerk. She counts the crates and customers, weighs their provisions, compares their ration tickets to their needs. Since the occupation, everything seems contaminated with the opposite of her husband's word.

At night in the kitchen, she runs short, not because he's a bad guy, but because he is good. Too good. His helpers in the store all cheat—he's caught them in the act—yet he won't allocate an extra portion to his own family. He won't take advantage. Enough is an abyss in which hope and reality disappear.

She starts off with a wedge of cheese on a cold November day. It's not much more than a rind and she chews it slowly. She helps herself to a handful of raisins later in the week. While cutting ham for a man with a paunch, she embezzles a tranche for her Saturday soup. She takes an apple or two, a scoop of peas, a gray bun, a bonus bit of lard, which she licks off her thumb. She steals, she pilfers—she devours. The only thing she considers enough these days is the duration of this horrible war.

Her husband detects discrepancies at times. She watches his honest hands tallying the tickets and measuring the flour sack on the scales. His hands work without ulterior motives, like they do on her body in the dark. She values his integrity, his refusal to give her more than his customers, more than her ration tickets allow, and her guilt is solid: She is a thief. But what she values even more is what's growing inside of her, this small, greedy, unnamed being whom she must protect from hunger at all cost.

What I Pack for a Sleepover at My Sister's House

- Gifts for the three of them so that the Frida Kahlo puzzle I picked up for Alina won't raise a flag; I have a bag full of non-bought presents, a mind full of her.
- A minimizing bra to downplay what's wrongly considered a symbol of my potentially upsetting fertility; for three years in our teens, my older sister's small breasts were larger than mine, but ever since hormones took over my body, I've carried twice the weight.
- The magazine that published my latest travel piece and must prove that I'm fulfilled, living like a nomad, don't crave what they have; my partner never committed, while my sister's did; they live like royalty in a row house with an excellent public school at walking distance.
- A pair of rubber boots so I can play with Alina in the yard even when it rains; the few precious hours we spend alone together must power me for months.
- Lipstick as pink as her birthday cake to make my feigned happiness more convincing; my sister's eggs never matured, while mine did.

- Chocolate truffles that are supposed to ban bitter questions from my tongue; could I have kept Alina? Could my brother-in-law (her father) and I have made a couple? Could I have anticipated how lawless my love for her would feel? Would I have asked my sister to become the generous auntie had our situations been reversed? Would I have brought in our mother as leverage? Would I have been able to live with myself had I said no? Would my sister still have been my sister?
- My reading glasses so I can read aloud the poem Alina will choose from the illustrated children's anthology I gave her soon after her birth; she always invites me to sit on her bed, her arm draped over my thighs like a casually abandoned doll; she often smiles at me, as though we share a secret.
- A flask of gin to remind myself, in the privacy of my sister's overly accommodating guest room, of the times she bailed me out in our twenties; it's pure magic that someone with a rotten side like me could have created something so sublime as Alina.
- The cooling eye mask that reduces swelling after tears; I'm forty-four now; it was already a stretch six years ago; even if the stars align in another dimension, they will never again form Alina.
- Earplugs so my ribcage won't blow apart when I'll hear my daughter cry for Mommy in the middle of the night.

Woman of the Century

Woman of the Century

At birth, she takes everything for granted. The impossible sky. Fleece to squeeze. A pair of tender green eyes that peers into hers each time she tests her voice. The plasticity of her mind, expanding, expanding.

When she turns ten, angst dominates. The world, apparently, doesn't revolve around her and she won't be loved for the goodness of her intentions. She becomes the girl who hangs back and sniffs the air, waiting for life to begin.

At twenty, she has it all figured out and writes her slogan on the wall. IT'S USELESS AND SILLY AND KIND OF NARCISSISTIC TO THINK OF YOUR LIFE AS BEING USELESS AND SILLY AND KIND OF NARCISSISTIC, BECAUSE THERE IS NO OTHER TYPE OF LIFE.

During the next decade, she meets regret. The man who decoded her turns out to be flawed. He considers "feminine" a synonym for "fake" and pokes holes through the pretensions she needs to believe in herself. She starts and stops drinking. Her life takes on the sour smell of missed opportunities.

At forty, she deals with ghosts. A green-eyed mother lost to cancer. Two miscarriages. A friend who fell (or jumped) off a cliff. Haunted by what-will-never-be, she watches her tears blur a page in a book on Pompeii. Fate is an accident for which nobody can be blamed.

In her fifties, she feels her second wind coming on. She's ready to dedicate herself and give more than she can miss. The air in her lungs, the blood in her veins, the thoughts still unvoiced in the hollows of her mind. If only the world, windswept and gray, could be a little less indifferent.

At sixty, she goes on a diet of culture and art, no longer bothering herself with the news. Politics is for people who are bored and, subsequently, boring. The people who take offense at her indifference ask her how she sleeps at night, knowing evil goes around unpunished. Well, she has known it for a very long time.

Turning seventy, she lives through a period of togetherness and exquisite tension. Smiles bounce back and forth between her and her lover at the breakfast table. They know how to be kind while staying on full sexual alert. Every day, toast and coffee lasts until noon.

At eighty, she becomes a minimalist. The present contains so much past that there's no more room for shallowness. She's not surprised when the monsters hiding beneath her bed take their leave. Not surprised yet disappointed. She must learn to sleep alone again.

In her nineties, she proliferates. Walks with the stumbling grace of a baby deer. Frowns with the gloominess of a retired judge. Laughs with the confidence of a skilled magician. Her friends, too, seem to multiply, then fall away, one by one.

Alone and dying, she maps out every hour, unable to locate herself. Have her ashes already been scattered? When death finally takes her away to a place beyond matter, her self dissolves and her ambiguous century ends.

MIRROR

The girl who yanks the yellow Hermès bag with my phone, keys, and cards off my shoulder in a quiet cobblestone street along an Amsterdam canal doesn't appear as innocent as the children stealing wallets on the café terraces near the old church, not as choreographed as the teenagers picking pockets on the squeaky tram, not as revengeful as my ill-chosen target five decades ago, but she's just as feisty as I was at her age, thirteen at most, and fierce like a stray cat while she tugs and tugs, avoiding my eyes at first, because it's better not to know the victim, better not to give remorse the chance to weaken your will, yet soon staring at me through the morning haze with amazement over how I keep the leather strap in my fist long enough to become a contender, someone who arouses her anger or perhaps admiration, because so few gray-haired women resist, and who catches her off guard by grasping her wrist and twisting it just so that she winces and feels forced to let go of my yellow bag, and who tells her in a surprisingly gentle voice that the path she's on is not worth it, that it will lead to scars like the one my revengeful target curved on my cheek, which isn't as ugly as it was in my youth, not as deterring a mark as I now need it to be, but which causes a sense of horror in the girl that pushes her beyond pity and into reflection, and when I release her fine wrist and she backs away from me slowly instead of bolting, I dare to believe that our day is off to a good start.

RIVALS

She arrives in the dark as though in response to my sigh, slipping into the room through a crack in the window. I stay in bed, unbelieving, but blood darts in my depths.

I sense more than see her presence, now here, then there, a leafy scent permeating the air, the sound of rustling dresses on a costumed ball.

My husband next to me dreams of my retirement, still decades away, our half-planned journey to Japan, my undivided attention. He hates waking up to an empty bed. The sheet is curled around his frame like a cocoon.

I know who she is, of course, having sighed her into existence: Daughter of memory, confidante of yearners like me.

"Come," I whisper, holding out my arms.

She hovers above my body and the breeze on my chest becomes a breath infused with her intentions. Her scent is sweeter than before, more like licorice, and my lips tingle as though expecting a kiss. But when I close my arms to embrace her, it's empty space I grasp. She cannot be forced. Unlike others in her realm, she was never raped and only touches those she chooses.

My husband mumbles in his sleep, twitches, jerks a leg. Is she touching him instead? I choke down my jealousy.

Before I can sigh again, she is on me, the unweight of her song brushing my breasts. Paper wings tickle my skin from shoulders to hands. I shiver. She fully enters me now, flits through my veins and flutters in my belly.

I lie still, greedy and giddy, absorbing as much of her as I can. When I finally rise from the bed, careful not to awaken my husband, I'm filled with more than I can name.

Retracing

It's easy to disappear in the dampness of Venice. Twelve moons ago, my mother wandered through a murky labyrinth of streets and bridges, crossing canal after canal—as I do now—leaving no footsteps. Cold air snakes across her face and her loneliness swells. She slips into a ruined palazzo like the fog at night and climbs the marble staircase. Music invites her to dance through the infinite ballrooms as the woman she once was. She twirls and forgets, shedding mass. She twirls and levitates. She is smoke, a cloud of perfume, vanishing into a dreamscape no mortal eye can see.

I blink. A cruise ship docks and its passengers inundate the streets. My mother stands stiff like a rock and lets the crowd flow around her like water. Her face goes taut from the scorn she harbors for group tourists, their stupidity, their loss of self. She imagines being mindless—no responsibilities, no decisions—and unexpectedly feels her body relax. Can she be a piece of driftwood instead of a rock? The lion of Saint Mark closes its eyes as she bobs along with the tourist flood, gaining a freedom she never knew existed. She buys, she sighs, she crosses the ramp. And when the monster ship cruises out of the harbor, she is gone.

One night, the alarm for the Aqua Alta sounds. I stand on the grand piazza as the water gurgles up from the drains and laps against my boots. The lagoon overflows, reaching for unbalanced life passing on the quays. My mother watches her reflection in the wrinkled surface and sees her dreams drown. The silt-streaked houses are silent; their windows, dead. She descends the quay's stone steps until the water whirls itself around her like a rope. Her heart sinks. The gondola floating by is as black as a coffin. I've read that people come to this dark, furtive town to become ghosts upon the sands of the sea.

What was I in her life, a ripple or a wave? What will happen to the memories she kept like tarnished secrets in her chest? Can she float into tomorrow without a body? What does my future weigh? Can I accept loss without knowing how it came to be? What is the essence of tears?

Stella Is

Stella is eight. She rubs a bowl between her legs, enjoying the smooth sweetness, until her mother snatches it away and tells her to behave.

Stella is fourteen. Her mouth is too hungry for words when she presses her hips against his.

Stella is eighty-seven. She lays her soft hand against his stubbled cheek and tells him it's okay to let go.

Stella is twenty. In control, exploring her own tight spaces. She moans, teetering on the edge of coming and building his excitement, until she rides out the crest of pleasure for them both.

Stella is thirty-three. Her breasts are as round as her belly, as he soap-massages her in the bath from clavicles to toes.

Stella is sixteen. She guides his hand between her legs, whispering about the forbidden bowl. But, no, she's not yet ready to meet that other part of him there.

Stella is fifty-two. On a skin-thin moment of delight, her nipples swell like buds in spring. The scent of sex grows on his chest all day.

Stella is thirty-nine. She pushes the twins on their garden twin swing, and with each rise of their little legs, her stomach lifts.

Stella is sixty-four. Retired, she gets a flying degree and takes him up in the air so he, too, can revel in weightlessness.

Stella is seventeen. He watches her parents bury her body—lifeless from an aneurysm—in the dress he bought for the night they had planned to share their first time.

Absent Reflections

I listen to all my selves, wild and unruly as they may be. I treat them with the patience and respect most of them lack. *How many ears must one woman have?* I sometimes ask them in front of the fireplace, quoting some poet or other. My selves talk all at once or interrupt one another or raise their voices or purposely whisper so softly that I must lean in to hear what they say.

Well, such is life in the castle, I guess. You must know how to take it and I usually do.

There are days, however, that I try to respond to my selves and find it hard to make them listen in return. They don't know who I'm speaking to or play at being ignorant. It would help, I suppose, if I knew their names and could address them individually. Unfortunately, they've never bothered to introduce themselves. They just appeared on my veranda one evening—no warning, no advance notice—and expected an invitation to come in. Lucky for them, I'm a generous person and curious, so I opened my double doors and gave them no trouble.

As you can imagine, they stayed. I offered each of them a chair at my table and a pillow in my bed and they made good use of both. It's on the chair where they do most of their talking, sharing their fears and fantasies, their failures and feats. In bed, staring at the ceiling, they silently contemplate themselves, or so I assume. Most are insomniacs and never dream. The few selves who love sleeping feel most at home during cold winter nights. I'm not sure why, but I can admire that.

Apart from the clamor at the table during meals, we tend to live together in harmony. We share the library and reception rooms, amble through the vinery and orchard, spook one another in the vaulted cellar. There's only one thing that truly hounds me, one thing that is many: their absent reflections. No matter how often I polish the mirrors in my hall, my selves refuse to show themselves. All I get as I pass are their shadows swiping the glass, shadows without depth and gradation amassing into one dark, indistinguishable blob.

Still, it's not enough of a nuisance for me to exile them outside the castle walls. I'm a generous person and curious and listen to all my selves.

OFFICE WOMEN

ONE

Maartje Dijkstra lives in a squeaky-clean apartment whose surfaces are scrubbed daily by the hands of others. Her legitimate excuse: She's allergic to dust, pollen, mold, hairs, and latex. At the high-rise office near the Rotterdam port, she works in a private cubicle with squeaky-clean linoleum floors and glass partitions. The rest of the insurance company is carpeted, because carpets don't scream when you walk all over them. Some employees get lost in the impersonal building, marching up and down the endless corridors, lost and not heard. But each time Maartje Dijkstra rolls her chair back or steps to her file cabinet on her rubber soles, her colleagues are notified and irritated. *Squeak, squeak* produces desk rage. They're even more irritated when she has a sneeze attack after having spent some time visiting the carpeted cubicles of others. Her indifference to their complaints—her allergies are not her fault—shows that Maartje Dijkstra could have been a big-time businesswoman with nerve and a taste for fancy clothes. In reality she's committed to her relationship with sugar and wears her work on her face, below her eyes, inside the pores of her tired skin. You can't tell from looking at her that she has known victory, that she once climbed the

Eiffel Tower stairs with six friends, wanting to arrive on top first and succeeding. At home, in her squeaky-clean apartment, she lives with her twelve-year-old daughter born from a marriage that lasted no longer than fourteen months. The ex-husband—she adored him—is a professional liability lawyer and amateur soliloquist. People say the other women never bothered Maartje Dijkstra. It was their odors he brought home with him on his skin. She is also allergic to perfumes.

TWO

Anke Vredenburg lives happily out of time. When she's at the Amsterdam headquarters unstapling reports for the board's meeting on EU lobbyists' regulations, she's simultaneously in Vondelpark underneath the large oak with the face of an owl grown into its bark. Feeling the papers slide through her fingers, she also feels the sharp edges of the grass with which she tends to play while reading Zweig, or Austen, or another author writing with a romantic touch on domestic life and death. When she later sits in Vondelpark for real, with her back against the oak's trunk, legs stretched out in front of her, and a novel in her hands, she concurrently finds herself at home at the kitchen table cutting into the body of a line-caught wild salmon that has been soaking in a marinade of citrus and ginger. The park's scent of pine needles effortlessly transmutes into the bitter taste of the fresh thyme she will add as a last-minute seasoning. At the kitchen table, she's already in bed, in bed she's already rinsing her hair, rinsing her hair, she's already Xeroxing papers for another bureaucratic hassle at headquarters. Each morning it's the same thing: waking up, unfurling herself, meeting the day. But Anke Vredenburg is known to beam after her first three cups of coffee. She flexes her face into a smile and freezes it as a dare—can you outdo my pleasantness? She may be a mousy woman, but she has charm. People say she never feels trapped in whatever moment she happens to find herself.

THREE

When Tessa van Wouden, former fundraising volunteer for Green Peace, starts working for Royal Dutch Shell, her friends think she has lost her mind. Or has she given up her dream to save the world? Not exactly. She's just tired of chasing the money and decides to work for it instead. Aware of the advantages her glorious body affords her, she goes from bed to bed, testing men some say, testing testicles. But she's not testing anything, she's merely contributing to the good cause. She seduces the rich and powerful and collects information to betray them to their wives, children, and superiors. She seizes the moral high ground before seizing what she can, blackmailing them into donations and charity. It's a lucrative strategy, sleeping with the hypocrites. Nobody wants their reputation damaged by perversity or illicit affairs, so they all rise to the bait. Under the patronage of Tessa van Wouden, Amnesty International flourishes. Although she suffers from self-loathing, she pursues her game in the interest of the world. The end justifies the means, right? Most suits don't seem quite human to her, and she never preys on the clean-cut boys, the ones with no dirty hands to hide. Her physical health, people say, is impeccable.

FOUR

1. Does Maartje Dijkstra enjoy the privacy her allergies afford her?

2. Can collectively picking on someone give colleagues a sense of solidarity?
3. Why did the ex-husband not try to sue the perfume companies?
4. Should Anke Vredenburg be described as having pale, dreamy eyes?
5. Can she claim a higher pay rate for working outside of regular hours?
6. Does her story take place in an office?
7. Are the seductions of Tessa van Wouden unethical?
8. Does she experience orgasms while at work?
9. If yes, are they unethical?
10. Are the three portraits told in the right order?
11. Would our three women sympathize with one another if they met?
12. Who has chosen the best escape?
13. What questions are missing from this survey?

Omission

For years, no one came to see me. I honestly didn't expect anyone would. My address is silent and my name erased. Human hope, though, is like taffy, and visitors are allowed. So I waited. I like to believe I would have given up waiting over time, but there's no way of knowing, because yesterday a child came to see me and left me her book. It's a blue scrapbook with pictures and poems she must have cut out from a multitude of sources. I like to imagine she completely ruined her parents' library. There's even a postmodern recipe for Dutch apple pie in the book and a drawing of an angry green mouse. I don't know who the girl is and I doubt she knows me. Perhaps we have both forgotten we met before, or we met in a parallel universe, or never. Not that it matters. What matters is that I don't deserve her book yet accepted it anyway. I didn't even show her sufficient gratitude. Kissing and touching is not allowed. The poems have proven useful in annoying my neighbors. They are something to recite during the long dark nights in which sleep never heals my wounds or those of my neighbors. The drawings are more difficult to share. I like to think they were tailor-made to compensate for my unique indistinct loss. Not that it matters. What matters is the life lesson omitted in the child's unexpected visit.

THE COST OF LIVING

Our six phones flatline before we arrive. The world that wears us down is out of reach. We alight from the car feeling airy and free. It's not our baggage that keeps us from floating; it's the weight of our steps on the flagstone path. We're heavy with resolve.

In the cabin we celebrate our joined solitude with root vegetables and bloody steaks—we're not innocent and don't pretend to be. We are brand strategists, personal finance consultants, media influencers, property lawyers, spin doctors, and market predictors. Still, our bubbly toast rings full of hope: Isolation plus focus equals victory. We will restore ourselves in peace and come home healthier, happier, more authentic. We say it's all about balance. The consumer economy cannot be to blame.

The closest village is over an hour drive down a rutted road. None of us want to leave the cabin and make the trip, so we postpone shopping for groceries. We're fine anyway. When we drove up the mountain, we brought a week's supply of produce and dried goods, and previous guests have left reserves in the cupboards. We invent dishes featuring canned tuna, falafel-mix, peanuts, and black-eyed peas. We wolf down jars of preserves. High from our bath salts, we sleep so deeply that we accuse one another of lacing the water with sedatives.

We think we know the cost of living.

When the snow begins to fall, we gaze in awe, as if delivered into a realm of myth. We go out and play, leaving our footprints on the white blanket, building elves with our bare hands. Snow is baby powder. Snow is cotton fluff. We devour all the butter as energy against the cold.

Much later, we will dig tunnels through the snow, though not for fun.

Our rental is not a jeep.

The snow doesn't stop by day, doesn't stop by night. It keeps falling, dwindling, swirling, boasting, disrupting. The blizzard turns the dark nights white and the afternoons gray. Peaches in syrup help, but not much. What do animals do when it snows? We are not survival savvy. None of us know how to trap or hunt.

We curse when the electricity goes out. While better for our detox, it's awful to watch our laptops die.

The mountain looks like an indifferent giant, carved in silence. Or like a cruel monster mocking our collapse: We're falling out of time, going from three meals a day to one light lunch.

We don't cheat. We don't sneak out at night to steal a snack. Believing that we're decent human beings makes us feel sated, we say. Besides, we can stand to lose some weight. Fasting is healthy and wasn't health one of our goals?

We sing at times, because six voices in harmony means we're in this together.

Our songs, however, sound like falling down a well in slow motion.

None of us understand how we've ended up on this side of the equation, where drinking instant coffee means having a feast.

Cold chews our bones in the dark.

Pizza, we say. Apple pancakes. Roast beef with mustard sauce. Smoked salmon on potato latkes. Grandmother's braised endives. The chocolate dessert the French make that's still liquid inside.

We disagree on whether it shows more strength to accept our situation as blind fate or to own up to our miscalculations and accept we're idiots.

We joke about burning the cookbooks once we run out of wood.

Our hunger mounts like a bill that we will have to pay.

While the blizzard rages, our muscles weaken. We calculate: how long the walk, how impossible the frozen, invisible route.

We turn to art for comfort, browse books, discuss subtitled films, take to drawing, pretend-recite poems, hit the piano keys. It's legal, we say, to cry in the face of art.

Our clothes grow and fear wraps itself around us like a robe. We're heading for that moment when despair finds a listener and is understood.

We drain our last crackers in sunflower oil and condensed milk. There's talk of walking out, walking away, speeding things up. Nightmares follow us around like ghosts. But we stay together, melting snow in the kettle on the iron stove. We lack the kind of courage we need to see ourselves as nothing.

When the dreaded day arrives, we gather in the kitchen and place our leftover edibles on the counter. Horseradish, dried onions, cloves, salt—a pointless army. With the reverence worthy of a ritual, we prepare the soup.

It's the first time for all of us to eat a last meal, and we eat it slowly, thinking that if we eat it slowly enough, we may never face the bottom of our bowls.

Then we lick our bowls, their bottoms. We lick the pan, thinking of grease.

Defeated, we watch the stove consume our air, the fuming flames still hungry. If the sky had been clear, the smoke rising from our chimney could have been a signal for help. We hallucinate the arrival of a miraculous stranger bringing oven-hot bread and hunks of moist cheese. Enough for everyone. Enough for the whole wide world.

LOOKING FOR A PLACE TO DIE

My memories and I sleepwalk into town, arm in arm, down the street of black stockings and long skirts, our flat heels *click-clacking* on the cobblestones. We pass the hat shop with its window of false promises behind which forgotten heroines change into child brides before our eyes. Horse carriages—the sting of dung— thunder by, so loud that talking to our sisters becomes impossible. We buy milk in glass bottles and are startled by the telephone that rings in the back room like a wayward alarm. With a forced smile, we pick up the horn and pronounce our name, which has strangely changed after we fell in love only once. On the street, the gas lamps have not yet been lit, so we continue along our way in the dusk, my memories and I, arm in arm, distracted by the questioning button eyes of our dolls; we close them at times to protect our dolls' hearts against the betrayal that is everywhere during the war. We step into a doctor's office, quickly, hesitant to take off our clothes, until we hear our own voice, screaming in childbirth. Breast cancer is not our fate. Neither is the dark closet of a teacher after school, although we're not too young to know of such things. At the end of town, we take a left, my memories and I, choosing a dark path where moths are courting one another and age threatens to crumble our bones.

We must have changed course, however, because soon early birds are circling in the sky again and spring turns its many green faces toward the sun. What a delight it is, we think, to live in a world in which you can witness the dawn multiple times a day.

Acknowledgements

This collection has been in the making for ten years and numerous people helped me along the way.

My thanks goes first to Marie Lamba, my agent: Your steady belief in me keeps me confident and creative. Thanks also to the wonderful people of Vine Leaves Press, my publishers Jessica Bell and Amie McCracken, my generous editor Melanie Faith, my copyeditor Melissa Slayton, and staff members who worked on this collection behind the scenes.

This book wouldn't have been possible without the feedback of fellow authors who commented on my stories before their publication. Forgive me for not mentioning everyone by name—you are too many—but I'd like to thank a few people in particular: Lynn Mundell, Jacqueline Doyle, Jolene McIlwain, Lisa Ferranti, Julie Zuckerman, Jennifer Kircher Carr, Corey Farrenkopf, and Gabrielle Griffis.

Thank you also to the readers who shared my work online or left me words of appreciation: Your encouragement means the world. Again, I cannot mention everyone by name, but must include several champions: Robin Flicker, Thaisa Frank, Kathy Fish, Sarah Freligh, Cathy Ulrich, Jonathan Cardew, Meg Tuite, James Tate Hill, Cheryl Papys, Tommy Dean, Jayne Martin, Pat Foran, Frances Gapper, Genia Blum, Jude

Marr, Emily Devane, Jan Stinchcomb, Tara Isabel Zambrano, Candace Hartsuyker, Dan Crawley, Patricia Bidar, Kathryn Kulpa, Dawn Miller, and April Bradley. Even if you don't see your name here, please know your support hasn't gone unnoticed.

For the love that fuels me as I write, I want to thank my family and friends: You inspire me every day even at a distance. Special thanks goes to Daniel, the man who knew I longed to write fiction before I could fully admit it to myself: I would not be who I am without you.

Last but definitely not least, I'd like to thank the editors and publishers of the literary magazines and anthologies in which my work previously appeared:

"Woman of the Hour" in *Fractured Lit*

"Dawn" in *Mid-American Review* (finalist for the Fineline Competition)

"Lost Animal Identities" in *Showcase Object/Idea*

"Playground," in *Bat City Review* (runner-up in Short Short Contest)

"Bleeding Girls Initiation Ritual" in *Monkey Bicycle*

"Speaking of Ovid" + "Double Life" in *Connotation Press*

"Her Face in the Glass" in *Flash: The Short Short Story Magazine*

"A Tasting of European Chefs" in *National Flash Fiction Anthology 2018*

"The Spider and I" + "New Leader" (selected for the Wigleaf Top 50) in *Cheap Pop*

"Copycat" in *SmokeLong Quarterly*

"Dance Partners" in *Pidgeonholes*

"The Next" in *Jellyfish Review*

"Swan Lake" in *Vestal Review*

"Classic" in *Whiskey Paper*

"Liabilities" in *Pithead Chapel*

"If You Think Stars Can't Clap, You're Not Listening" in *National Flash Fiction Anthology 2021*

"Woman of the Week" and "Woman of the Century" in *matchbook*

"Battle of Brushes" + "Lost and Found" in *Atticus Review*

"Floris, Fate, and The Friendly Stranger" in *Spelk Fiction*

"Ugly Thing" + "Retracing" in *New Flash Fiction Review*

"The Hardest Thing" in *Iron Horse* (finalist in the Flash Fiction Competition)

"Woman of the Year" in *Wigleaf*

"Five Forbidden Friends" in *Fictive Dream*

"The Mind Reader" in *Hobart*

"Guillotine" (as "The Guillotine Reinvented") in *Little Fiction*

"Closed Circle" in *The Sunlight Press*

"Attic" (as "Limbo Land") in *Lost Balloon*

"Inner Thief" in *FlashBack Fiction*

"Mirror" in *Cincinnati Review*

"Stella Is" in *The Mambo Academy of Kitty Wang* and *Best Microfiction 2021*

"Absent Reflections" (as "The Hall of Mirrors") in *PopShot*

"Office Women" in *Necessary Fiction*

"The Cost of Living" in *The Rupture* (then called *The Collagist*)

"Looking for a Place to Die" in *Atlas and Alice*

www.ingramcontent.com/pod-product-compliance
Ingram Content Group UK Ltd.
Pitfield, Milton Keynes, MK11 3LW, UK
UKHW012253290726
14090UKWH00016B/618

9 783988 321633